"We haven't even finished your tree."

Tyler inched closer to Kate, his body pressed up against hers, sending all sorts of delightful signals.

"I'm going to kiss you now," he told her, and although she opened her mouth to protest, not one word came out as his lips touched hers.

Kate had never been kissed like this before. Kissing Tyler was like a mind-altering drug. She was losing control—fast. She'd known the man only twenty-four hours, yet it was as if she'd wanted him her entire life.

Why was it that the man you couldn't have permanently was the one who kissed the best?

The Christmas Date

MICHELE DUNAWAY

HARLEQUIN® AMERICAN ROMANCE®

Recycling programs
for this product may
not exist in your area.

ISBN-13: 978-0-373-75501-1

THE CHRISTMAS DATE

Copyright © 2007 by Michele Dunaway

Printed in U.S.A.

ABOUT THE AUTHOR

In first grade **Michele Dunaway** knew she wanted to be a teacher when she grew up, and by second grade she knew she wanted to be an author. By third grade she was determined to be both, and before her high school class reunion, she'd succeeded. In addition to writing romance, Michele is a nationally recognized, award-winning English and journalism educator who also advises the yearbook, newspaper and student website at her school. Born and raised in a west county suburb of St. Louis, Missouri, Michele has traveled extensively, with the cities and places she's visited often becoming settings for her stories.

Chapter One

Tyler Nichols was a man used to being stared at.

At six foot three, with dark brown hair and a cheeky smile that some women claimed was almost as sexy as Brad Pitt's, Tyler attracted the ladies the way nectar drew honeybees.

But the leggy brunette giving him the once-over didn't have a chance of holding his interest this morning. Nor did a redhead as he strode on by, his expensive, though well-worn, leather camera case slung over his shoulder.

Tyler grimaced as a burly man brushed by him and bullied his way to the front of the line, as if being first meant he would get to the baggage-claim area faster. Perhaps the guy hadn't learned everyone waited for the people movers at Orlando International Airport.

Welcome back to America, land of the Hurry, Hurry, Hurry, It's All About Me mentality. Tyler glanced at his watch and grinned. Maybe the man had an early meeting and his flight had landed late. Tyler was actually ahead of schedule; no one expected him until December 3.

"That guy was pushy, wasn't he?"

Tyler turned around, letting his brown-eyed gaze

rove over the striking redhead who had followed him into the train. She smiled, shooting him all the right signals, but then again, she didn't know she was in the wrong place at the wrong time. Any unmarried man would be interested, but unfortunately for her, romantic dalliances weren't anywhere near the top of Tyler's list today. He'd spent the past three months in Iraq, and today he had places to go and work to attend to—like the stacks of mail that had piled up during his overseas assignment. So he gave the redhead a nonchalant shrug and gripped the steel pole as she moved away, quickly masking her disappointment in his lack of interest.

Moments after announcements in both English and Spanish told passengers to stay clear of the closing doors, the train whisked passengers toward their luggage. Tyler took a moment to reflect on the work he had done in Iraq. Maybe a Pulitzer Prize awaited him for his photographs from Iraq. Perhaps this upcoming year he would receive the accolades that had so far eluded him.

In the more than eleven years he'd been a news photographer, Tyler had been through wars, natural disasters and presidential elections. He'd covered coups, uprisings and Oscar celebrations. He'd crawled on his belly through underbrush, gone without bathing for days and even once trekked into the heart of the South American rain forest, as mysterious as ever but unfortunately, rapidly disappearing.

Women were drawn by his exotic job, until they realized that he wasn't the type to settle down. He kept no pets or plants, and rented a one-bedroom apartment.

Well, he used to rent an apartment. Now, thanks to his twin sister, Tyler was a home owner. He'd bought the place sight unseen two months ago, giving his sister power of attorney to make the purchase. She'd sent him a text message once the deed was done.

He hadn't really wanted the responsibility of a house. To him, owning one reeked of permanence. But his accountant and his lawyer sister had insisted that Tyler needed the mortgage-interest deduction for his taxes. They'd convinced him that buying a home was a better long-term investment than buying a condominium.

His twin must have done a good job, because Tyler's mother had e-mailed him that she'd found his new place charming. Of course she added that she hoped it was a "step in the right direction"—in other words, that he was settling down.

The train came to a smooth stop and Tyler allowed the others to exit first, including the redhead, who gave him one last glance. He readjusted his camera bag and once again ignored her, too busy contemplating the tasks ahead.

KATE MERRILL was running late. Since her boss would be in court all morning, Kate had set her alarm for an extra half hour of sleep. What she hadn't intended was for the alarm clock to malfunction and not ring at all. She'd woken up more than an hour late, showered and thrown herself together in less than twenty minutes. The moment she'd turned the key in her car, she'd remembered her fuel gauge was on empty.

She pulled into a gas station and her compact car sputtered to a stop. She glanced at the clock on the dash before hopping out. Nine-fifteen. She was supposed to pick up those depositions at the opposing counsel's law firm at nine-thirty. If the traffic gods were kind, she just might make it.

She swiped her credit card, cursed that even bottom-grade unleaded gas was up ten cents for the third time in two weeks, and wondered how the guy in the Hummer on the other side of the pump could afford the behemoth he was driving.

And didn't he know how bad those vehicles were for the environment? Sighing, Kate positioned the hose in the gas tank and went to clean her windshield. Her wiper blades needed replacing and last night's winter rain had been mostly drizzle, meaning her windshield was dusty. The temperature had been wacky lately, as well, likely due to global warming caused by whoever was driving the beast on the other side of her. He or she probably got only fifteen miles to the gallon, whereas Kate averaged at least twenty-five on a good day—which this was turning out *not* to be. At least she didn't have too far to go to reach the other lawyer's office. Of course, after that she'd have another half-hour drive back to the law firm of Murray, Evans and Jasper, where she'd been working as Marshall Evans's paralegal since graduating from college five years ago. She hoped no one had noticed she hadn't made it in this morning as she had been scheduled to.

Kate resisted the urge to curse as she found an empty container where the squeegee should have been. She glanced over to the next bucket. Nothing in that one, either. Great. She stepped between the pole and the pump, checking to see if the Hummer's driver had the windshield-cleaning wand. He did, and as he turned from lowering his driver's-side wiper blade, Kate froze.

The man in front of her was tall—at least six feet to

her five foot five. His closed lips were full and perfect. His hair was dark and silky and curled at his nape. He needed a haircut, but like a rock star, he could get by without one—the shagginess added character. His chest, under a short-sleeved maroon polo shirt, was broad and toned. Light hair dusted his forearms. He was, as the girls in the office would say, to die for.

He seemed to sense she was staring, because he frowned and said, "Uh, can I help you?"

Kate cringed. She knew what he saw: pale skin lacking any natural Southern suntan, dark blond hair confined in the tight knot she always wore to work. She was nothing special at all.

Unlike him.

She gathered her composure, determined to show him how unaffected she was. After all, he probably had the ego to match his looks. Guys like him always did.

"Are you done with that?" She arched an eyebrow and pointed to the black plastic object in his hand.

"Yeah. Sure." He gave her a bemused look and held out the handle. Kate's fingers accidentally brushed his as she took the squeegee from him.

"Thanks." She turned to dip the sponge in the washer fluid then began to clean her front windows.

In the meantime, the pump clicked off, signaling her tank was full. She hadn't heard the Hummer's pump shut off, but she assumed it had, since the man had disappeared into the gas station, presumably to pay.

She finished the front windshield and did the back, as well, figuring that late was late, as her boss would say, and he'd much rather have her safe than injured in an accident because she'd been unable to see.

Kate tossed the squeegee back in the bucket. While

she loved her job as a paralegal, her goal was to be a lawyer and she'd devoted herself these past five years to earning a law degree in night school. Marshall had already offered her a position as an associate lawyer upon her graduation next spring, and while Kate was grateful he'd made her job search easier, she hadn't yet said yes. Murray, Evans and Jasper was one of Orlando's largest firms, and that meant dozens of people worked there, many of whom Kate had never met. She couldn't discount her concern that she might be more comfortable starting out in a smaller firm. Although the anonymity of a large firm might help her when she showed up late—as she would today.

Her receipt printed, and she tore it off, but as she did so, the wind tugged it from her grasp and sent it flying across the station lot.

She started after it as fast as her sensible one-inch blue pumps would allow. She had almost retrieved it when a hand reached down to the pavement and scooped up the wayward slip. "Here you go."

Him.

"Uh, thanks." He placed the paper in her waiting hand, his touch almost ticklish against her palm. She closed her hand around the slip, crumpling the paper, and straightened. "I appreciate your help."

"You're probably someone who reconciles receipts with your credit-card statement," he said.

"Is there something wrong with that?" Kate snapped, irritated at the day and this man, who'd somehow pegged her when he didn't even know her. Worse, he was smiling!

"Of course not," the guy said with a grin. "Have a

great day and watch those receipts. They like to escape."
Then he climbed into the black Hummer.

Kate stood there a moment, fuming as she watched
him drive out of the gas station. Then she shook herself. Yes, those hot guys were all the same. Arrogant.
Cocky. Self-assured. Jack had been that way— No, she
wouldn't think of Jack the Jerk. And she wouldn't think
about this guy. Orlando, Florida, was a huge place. It
wasn't as though she'd see him again.

Thank goodness.

"You know, finding Mr. Right is like riding a horse.
If you fall off, you have to climb right back into the
saddle."

Kate stared at her best friend and coworker, who'd
stopped by. Up until this moment, her day had gotten
better. Marshall's court appearance had been success-
ful, and no one had said anything about her not getting
to the office until ten.

"That's not it. I have to study tonight," Kate said,
trying to explain why she didn't want to attend Gail's
party. "I've got finals in a few weeks."

Wendy exhaled, causing a strand of her wavy brown
hair to dance. "Study tomorrow. That's what Saturday
afternoons are for. Tonight you need to get out and find
a new man."

Kate sighed. Three years of close friendship meant
that Wendy wouldn't give up. The two women were the
classic example of opposites attract. Wendy was a viva-
cious brunette; Kate a blonde who'd rather study than
socialize. Wendy dated three to five times weekly; Kate
dated that number yearly.

"Wendy," Kate began. "I'm tired of people thinking

there's something wrong with me just because I don't have a man in my—"

Wendy cut Kate off with an emphatic shake of her head. "Well, I'm tired of your excuses. Just because you live on a street populated with retirees doesn't mean you have to be old before your time. Heck, most of the seniors on your block probably have a better sex life than you do. When's the last time you got any action? And don't tell me it was Jack."

"Wendy!" Kate remonstrated and glanced around her cubicle. Hopefully no one had overheard her. Kate had been embarrassed enough already.

"Seriously, Kate. The guy was a jerk. We all told you not to date him, and ever since he, well…"

Wendy paused and Kate grimaced as she thought of Jack's public dumping of her, where, in front of no fewer than ten people, he declared her to be a cold fish.

"Don't say it," Kate warned. Despite the incident having taken place over half a year ago, the humiliation was still fresh.

"Fine. But you're closeting yourself away. Men are good for something, you know."

Yeah, catching receipts, Kate thought as she frowned. She'd learned the hard way that men, especially attractive men, simply weren't interested in her. She was too plain, too uptight, too smart, too career-focused, too something.

Men were like roadwork zones. You had to use extreme caution. Besides, she'd never been good at dating. Maybe her inadequacy stemmed from her mother's abandonment. Perhaps Kate was simply the ice maiden Jack had declared her to be. He'd called her the most frigid woman he'd ever been to bed with. She could still picture everyone's shocked faces.

"Stop thinking about it," Wendy said, reading Kate's mind. "Your mom and Jack both did a number on you. But only you can break the victim cycle."

"I understand that, which is why I refuse to be like her or deal with guys like Jack again. Dating can wait. My priority is graduation from law school then a career. Then maybe a husband. Unlike my mother, who had too many boyfriends to count and three marriages lasting mere months, I'm planning on doing it only once. Heck, maybe I'll be like Oprah and not get married. Besides, I'm one step ahead. I've already got the house."

"Yeah, on a street where the average age is a hundred. You're twenty-seven." Wendy pursed her lips. "You're still young. Give men another chance to prove they aren't all like Jack. At least get out there and mingle. No one's saying you have to marry the next man you meet. Just indulge your needs a little. A woman has them. Believe me, I know."

"You indulge yours all the time," Kate said, cracking a smile. She'd heard all the stories, usually over morning coffee, when Wendy would regale Kate with her previous night's adventures.

Kate's reply threw Wendy off balance, but only for a second. Wendy grinned. "You bet I do. Who says a man should be the only one to play the field? There's a huge double standard. I'm worried that if you don't, you'll forget how. Then you'll end up an old maid with just your devil cat for company until the end of your days."

"My cat is not a devil," Kate rebuked. Her cat was merely temperamental, that was all. "And remember my mantra. There are worse things than being alone. Jack was perfect proof."

"I'm sure you're not what he said, but you won't prove to yourself that you weren't the cause of his erectile dysfunction until you get back out there. The cure for your tension is a night of unbridled lust." Wendy saw the dubious expression on Kate's face. "Okay, some harmless flirtation. Platonic. Jeez. And speaking of that house, perhaps you should move someplace more happening. My condo complex, for example, would be perfect. Not a retiree in sight."

Wendy's condo complex had the nickname Sin City—it was full of young singles and full of sin. Kate rolled her eyes. "My grandmother willed me the house. It's paid for. Already the property value has gone up ten percent. It's a good investment."

Wendy was not to be daunted. "Exactly! She'd want you to sell and invest the money. Buy yourself some slinky clothes, get a hip condo and find a nice man to warm your bed. I'm sure your grandmother didn't want you to live alone and celibate on a street full of geriatrics who have retired to central Florida for fun in the sun. Stop suppressing your sexuality. I mean, when was the last time you kissed someone?"

Forever. The image of the guy at the gas station jumped into Kate's head again and she slumped. As if such a guy would ever consider her.

"Look, I'm not like you," she said softly. Men of all types flocked to Wendy and she went through them like candy, claiming she quickly got bored. "I grew up on that street," Kate continued, "I'm comfortable there. I'm busy with school, and most law-school grads are younger than I am. They didn't opt for the night-school-takes-forever plan. I have to be competitive, so my grades are important."

"You know I only want what's best for you. As a friend of long standing, I have to tell you you're becoming isolated. You're losing touch."

"Well, Nora does always drop hints for me to date her grandson, Niles," Kate conceded.

Wendy scoffed. "Yeah, right. Any grandson of Nosy Nora is bound to be a geek."

Perhaps, and Kate didn't want to date Niles any more than she wanted to date someone else. Seeing Kate's silence as indecision, Wendy overrode Kate's last defense.

"Kate, today is November thirtieth. You can put off studying for one night, especially since it's the weekend. Get out and live a little. Hang out with all your friends. We've missed you, me in particular."

"Wendy…" Kate said.

Her friend stood firm. "Kate, you cannot base every guy on Jack the Jerk. I know he hurt you, but put it behind you. We'll have fun."

Kate picked up the troll doll she kept on her desk and gave him a vicious twirl. His orange hair spiked. Although the idea didn't sit well, maybe she did need to pick up a man she didn't care about and do the deed, just see if the lack of passion had been more Jack's fault than hers. And she *had* missed hanging out with her friends. "Fine. I'll go."

"Super." Wendy smiled now that the matter was settled. "I'll pick you up at eight. Be ready. Wear something sexy." With that, Wendy headed for the elevator. Kate stood up, peered over the cubicle walls and watched her walk away.

"Eight o'clock," Wendy called as the elevator doors opened. "Don't forget."

"I won't." Kate slumped back in her chair, ready to put her lack of a love life behind her and get back to work.

"GIN."

As Nora spread her winning hand on the card table, revealing the jack of clubs Frieda needed, Frieda tossed hers down in disgust. She'd been playing cards with Nora for over thirty years, but she'd never been beaten this bad by her best friend and neighbor, the self-titled Queen of Dogwood Lane. "That's the sixth time in a row," Frieda said, miffed about her current winless streak. This was supposed to be a fun way to relax after helping Nora put up her Christmas decorations. No one was as serious about Christmas as Nora; she had everything up by the end of November.

"I can't help that I'm a winner. When you're hot, you're hot." Nora grinned, the smile lines at her mouth deepening.

Frieda snorted and reached for her cup of spiced tea. While good, it wasn't as cinnamon-y as hers. "You haven't been hot in over forty-five years. Now, if you want hot, I've heard that a single man is moving into our neighborhood."

"You're so far behind. You heard right and I knew that months ago," Nora said. She considered herself not only the mistress of Dogwood Lane's grapevine, but the Neighborhood Watch leader, as well. She shuffled the cards. "Myra's granddaughter told me who bought it."

Frieda arched a gray eyebrow and waited as Nora dealt another game. "You have to admit that this is exciting news. We haven't had a single man on this street in years. I mean, not counting Elmer. He's eighty. I heard the new guy is thirty-three. Maybe our block will become hip again."

"Doubtful. The only new hip around here is Sue Ellen's artificial one."

"So what do you think he looks like?" Frieda asked. Sue Ellen's surgery was old news.

Nora shrugged. "Not as good as my Niles, I'm sure."

Frieda refrained from rolling her eyes. Everyone on the block knew that Nora worshipped the ground her middle grandson walked on. Although her own children declared her more of a meddler, Nora had managed to get two of her six grandchildren hitched.

All of Nora's children were scattered around the country, and Niles lived closest. Nora usually traveled over the Christmas holidays to visit everyone, but this year everyone, including Niles, was coming to Orlando. So he'd be in town in a little less than four weeks.

Frieda peered at her cards. "Wouldn't it be great if the new neighbor and Kate hit it off? She's been so lonely since Sandra died two years ago, and well, you remember how disastrous her last relationship was. Who knows? Perhaps it'll be love at first sight with the boy next door."

It was Nora's turn to scoff. "Absolutely not. The last thing Kate needs is some guy who will break her heart again. She should date Niles. He's perfect for her."

"He lives in Jacksonville," Frieda pointed out.

"So? They have lawyers in Jacksonville, too, I'm sure."

Frieda managed not to shudder as she drew a card from the pile. While Nora was an avid matchmaker and

Frieda often assisted in her schemes, Frieda's gut said *no way* to Niles and Kate as a couple.

Nora removed the queen of spades from the discard pile and added it to her hand. "Sandra would approve of Niles. He's a nice, hardworking boy with a very good job."

Sandra had raised Kate ever since her mother had dropped her off when she'd been six, and Frieda was positive Sandra would turn over in her grave first before agreeing. Still, Frieda could hope that maybe the new guy would be perfect for Kate. After all, Frieda and Nora had promised Sandra when she'd first gotten ill that they'd look after Kate. Of course, Nora was starting to think that meant Kate should be married off.

Frieda glanced out the window and across the street. Both houses, Kate's and the new neighbor's, remained dark. "When's he arriving, anyway?" Frieda asked.

Nora frowned. "That I don't know. I heard he's a photojournalist who's always jaunting off somewhere. The moving van arrived weeks ago and unloaded, so his stuff's there. If he doesn't show up soon, his house will be the only one on the block without holiday decorations. That would be an eyesore."

Frieda studied her cards. If she drew the two of clubs she'd win. "Maybe he'll be as sexy as that Arthur Kent. Remember him from the first Gulf conflict?"

"Of course I remember that far back. I had cable long before it was fashionable. You really should move into this century. Anderson Cooper's the star now. Gin. So, where do you think Niles should take Kate? The theater? Ballroom dancing? *The Nutcracker* will be in town for a limited run starting next week."

Or none of the above, if she's lucky—unlike me,

Frieda thought as she tossed her cards down, defeated again. Nora peered over her cat-eye rims. "Well?"

"Uh…" Frieda stalled. Everyone knew how tenacious Nora was. Somehow Frieda would have to help Kate get out of this one. Behind the scenes, that is. "Why don't you let Kate decide what she wants?"

After all, December 1 would initiate twenty-five days of pure holiday magic. With a little mistletoe and a lot of Christmas joy, who knew what could happen?

TYLER DOUBLE-CHECKED the directions his sister had text-messaged him a month ago. The quaint neighborhood he now drove through wasn't quite what he'd expected.

Not that it was bad or that he disliked it. He'd just expected something newer and more modern, not the starter bungalows he was passing on street after street with fifty-year-old trees. This neighborhood was located in an older part of town, built long before theme parks had transformed everything in Orlando and moved the hub of the city to the southwest. Tyler crept along, searching for 233 Dogwood Lane.

There it was. Home sweet home.

He parked his Hummer under the carport. Admittedly, the SUV was a monstrous gas guzzler, but Tyler wasn't around enough to drive the beast much. In the two years he'd owned the vehicle, he'd put less than three thousand miles on his odometer.

Except for the unkempt yard, the house itself was presentable—and just like every other rectangular abode on the street. The two-to three-bedroom homes were early 1950s and painted shades of cream or white. All the houses had Christmas decorations on the lawn, some more abundantly than others.

Tyler exited his vehicle, stood in the driveway and glanced around the neighborhood, which he'd been pleased to discover wasn't a traffic-jammed drive from the downtown bureau office. He reminded himself it didn't matter what his house looked like. He'd live in it, on average, maybe a total of three months a year.

He dug out the key his sister had mailed to his P.O. box and blinked. Had the blinds across the street flickered? He shook his head. Perhaps it had been a trick of the waning sun or the Christmas lights competing with the twilight. He steadied himself and reminded himself he was back in America, one of the safest countries in the world.

He took a deep breath. Aside from being tired and jet-lagged, he was still jumpy from having been in a place where gunfire was routine. The key turned easily and the side door creaked open. Once inside, Tyler nudged the door shut and flipped on the overhead light. As he set down his camera case, disturbed dust particles rose into the stagnant air. Tyler's expression soured. He knew his stuff had been delivered weeks ago, but he hadn't expected the dust to be this bad. A thin layer covered everything, including the moving boxes. Which meant that not only did he have to unpack, he first had to clean.

That figured, especially since he hated housekeeping and had entrusted his apartment to a cleaning service. Since Tyler hadn't been in the country for the various home-owner inspections, he'd simply assumed the previous owners had scoured the place. Used to living in apartments, where a renter had to clean to get his deposit back and then the apartment complex cleaned to prepare for the new tenant, Tyler hadn't even thought his house might not be habitable.

He stretched his neck and rolled his shoulders in an attempt to ease the tension he felt. From the appearance of the place, the movers had simply brought all his stuff in, set it down and then left. He'd slept in more deplorable conditions on the job, but this was his house. His home, even though he was never home much, was a haven, one he always wanted clean and presentable.

He pulled his cell phone out of the camera bag and punched speed dial. Within moments he'd connected to his twin's voice mail. "Hey, Tara. Thanks for remembering the cleaning service. I couldn't believe how spotless the house was when I got home. Gosh, everything in its place and not a speck of dust anywhere. Hey, on a serious note, I'm back in town and I do like the house. You did good. Love ya. Call me."

He smiled, imagining her reaction to the first part of his message. She'd known him since the womb and would laugh at his sarcasm, aware it was only in jest. Yeah, he was annoyed by the mess in front of him, but it wasn't her fault. She'd already gone above and beyond the call of sisterly duty.

The house was too dirty not to clean, but because he'd always had a maid service, wiping up spills with paper towels and spraying foaming shower cleaner were his limits. He didn't even own a vacuum, since the service had brought its own.

For a moment, he thought about calling his mother, then reconsidered. While she could clean at light-speed, her help would come with a lecture on staying in the United States, finding a woman to marry and raising children, like two of his older brothers, Leo and Craig. Tonight, after traveling a long distance and then working all day at the office, Tyler wanted peace and quiet.

The sound of tires crunching on pavement caught his attention. He moved to the front window and watched as a sensible little four-door sedan pulled into the driveway next door. He strode to a side window and parted the old-fashioned Venetian blinds. Once under the carport, the vehicle sputtered to a stop. Clogged fuel injector. Easy enough to fix.

The car door opened and the driver climbed out. No. It couldn't be. What were the odds?

He frowned. But there she was, the woman who, for some reason, he'd been unable to get out of his mind.

Maybe it had been the severe way she'd secured her blond hair in a bun, or the way she'd haughtily held her neck and shoulders, as if he carried the plague. He'd made a career of never forgetting a face, but clearly she wasn't very observant. She'd failed to notice the Hummer parked parallel to her driveway, and seemed preoccupied with getting into the house as quickly as possible.

Curiosity piqued, Tyler decided it was time to formally meet his new neighbor.

Chapter Two

As she entered her kitchen, Kate tossed her keys on the table and set the pint-size carton of Ben & Jerry's ice cream in the freezer. She'd eat the chocolate, caramel and fish-shaped-candy ice cream later. Because of a last-minute request from the boss, she'd left work a little later than normal, which was okay, she'd rationalized, since she'd arrived late.

Still, she hadn't factored the horrible traffic an accident had produced, which had left her with the task of getting dinner, freshening up and finding something to wear in a little less than the two hours she had before Wendy arrived.

Kate had the start of a headache, as well, and something seemed out of place, though she couldn't pinpoint what. Maybe she was just tense from the day, and the fact she'd agreed to go to a party she really didn't want to attend.

She took two acetaminophen tablets out of her purse, poured a glass of water and shrugged off the melancholy as her cat, Jeckyll, hopped onto the kitchen table with a meow. Tonight Kate didn't scold him, for Wendy's prophetic words popped into Kate's head: *you'll end up an old maid with just your cat.* Kate swallowed the tablets, set the water glass down and absently scratched Jeckyll behind the ears.

The huge yellow tomcat arched his back and purred. Then he rose on his hind legs and planted his two huge front feet on Kate's blouse. Dirty paw prints instantly marred the white fabric above her breasts. Figured. Her headache grew worse as she grabbed a paper towel and attempted to wipe the dirt off the material. Because she'd watered the plants late last night, brushing the dirt off was hopeless. She needed to toss the garment into the washing machine immediately.

"Bad cat! I told you to stay out of the corn plant," she chastised. She began unbuttoning the blouse as Jeckyll jumped off the table and nonchalantly strode into the living room, tail held high. Kate glared after him, fingers freezing on undoing the fourth button as she heard a knock on the side door.

Probably Nora. Kate closed her eyes for a moment. She loved Nora—the woman was practically her second mother. But at this moment Kate was simply too uptight to deal with anyone.

The rapping continued and Kate went to the door. She flipped on the porch light and slowly pushed the curtain aside so that Nora, head of the Neighborhood Watch patrol, wouldn't scold her—again—for not being careful enough. "Yes?"

The rest of her sentence died on her tongue. Outside on her doorstep was the guy from the gas station. She dropped the curtain. What was he doing here? Every one of Nora's safety lectures flitted through Kate's head. Had he followed her all day? Should she call 911?

The knocking restarted, this time accompanied by his voice, which called, "Hello." She pushed the curtain aside again, and he gave her a disarming grin and held up his driver's license. "Hi. I'm your new neighbor. I bought the house next door. From the Dorhacks?"

Kate's hand trembled as she let the curtain drop into place. She chided herself for letting Nora's paranoia rub off. She opened the door and immediately noticed the massive black Hummer directly on the other side of her carport. Okay, maybe she was as clueless as Nora maintained if she'd missed that. Somehow, she regained her voice and poise. "Hello."

"Hi. I'm Tyler Nichols."

She blushed. "Kate Merrill."

He smiled and something inside her jumped to attention. "I've been in Iraq for the past few months," he said. "Just got home today. Pity we didn't know each other this morning."

"Oh." She gripped the door handle. Even though he stood lower than her, his height put him eye-to-eye, providing her a clear view of brown orbs that were flecked with gold. She swallowed. "Well, welcome to Dogwood Lane."

The smile didn't fade as he studied her. "Thanks. What a coincidence."

Kate sidestepped the comment. "Uh, so you were working overseas?" she managed to say.

He nodded, and the dimple in his cheek creased more. "I'm a photojournalist with a wire service."

Gorgeous man, glamorous job. And not only had she made an idiot of herself this morning, but now she was leaving him standing on her doorstep. "Uh, please come in. Besides, if you remain out here, Nora'll be here any second."

He frowned. "Nora?"

"Nora," Kate confirmed as another strand of her hair escaped its bun when she stepped back into the kitchen. She resisted the urge to replace the wayward lock. "You'll meet her soon enough. She lives across the street and keeps a pair of binoculars by each window. Everyone in the neighborhood calls her Nosy Nora. Not to her face, of course," Kate added hastily, blushing again. "Some twenty years ago she foiled a crime on this street, so everyone's very grateful she's observant."

He was observant, too, she noticed as his gaze flicked around her kitchen, which sorely needed updating. The green metal cabinets had gone out of style decades ago. He returned his attention to her face.

"I'm sure you're busy, especially since it's a Friday night. I just came over to say hello. I've got to get back over there and clean."

"You're not going out?" Kate stared at him. Didn't men like him always have somewhere exciting to be? Jack had always had somewhere to go, someone to impress.

But Tyler was shaking his head. "No. I've got hours of work to do, starting with finding the closest place to buy cleaning supplies."

"We're pretty residential here. You'll have to drive at least two miles before you get to the nearest superstore," Kate told him.

He grinned wryly. "That's what I figured. Well, I'm sure I'll be seeing you around. I better get to it. I recognized you and like I said, I just wanted to say hello."

He could charm without even trying. His proximity rattled her brain, scattering her priorities and overriding her to-do list. Maybe she should have taken Wendy's advice and gotten on the dating circuit sooner. That might have helped with her reaction to this man.

"I saw the inside of the house right after Myra's kids put her in a nursing home. They were so happy to unload the place that I'm not surprised they didn't clean it before they sold it."

"Well, my stuff sitting there collecting dust didn't help. I've been traveling with a marine unit for the past two months. Although, as dirty as it is, it's better than the front line."

Raised by Sandra always to be charitable and volunteer, Kate made an instinctive decision. "Do you need some help?"

His eyebrows shot up. "You'd do that?"

"Of course," she said. "It's what neighbors do, especially on this street. I've got tons of cleaning stuff I can lend you. Give me a few minutes to get changed and I'll come over. I'd suggest you find some grubbier clothes."

He still seemed a little surprised. "Okay, if you're sure. I'll see you in a few then. Be sure to knock loud. I've discovered that the doorbell's broken. I guess I'll have to fix that at some point."

And then he walked away, affording Kate a great view of his backside.

So that was his next-door neighbor.

Tyler whistled to himself as he crossed the short distance to his house. The spontaneous way she'd offered to help, without hitting on him, had impressed him. Perhaps he'd misjudged her this morning. Then, he'd found her a bit amusing.

Oh, she still had that naiveté to her, as real as it was refreshing. But her eyes reflected intelligence. He'd read determination on her face. She'd never play poker, but she'd covered her shock well.

He'd also found it intriguing that he'd wanted to pull her hair out of that infernal bun she wore. Yeah, maybe he'd been without a woman for too long, because his male interest had roared to life the moment she'd opened the door. He chuckled. Those sexy paw prints on her chest had been pretty impressive. Lucky cat. He wondered if she realized the top part of her blouse had been unbuttoned, giving him a nice peek at the white satin bra she wore beneath. Since his mother had raised him a gentleman, Tyler had kept his gaze on her face, but it hadn't been easy.

Fate had to have a sense of humor. The first flare of life his libido had felt in a long time was for his next-door neighbor, a slip of a girl who, from her wary expression, wasn't too impressed with him in the slightest, especially if this morning was an indication.

Not that it mattered. He'd always maintained that one should not seduce one's neighbor. That rule was part of Tyler's personal set of commandments for his life. Getting involved in a relationship with your neighbor made life awkward afterward, even if one neighbor— him—would never be in town. He'd learned that lesson the hard way.

Which was too bad. Because Kate Merrill had potential.

KATE CLOSED the door, picked up Jeckyll and shook her head. Darn it all. What in the world had gotten into her? She'd just offered to clean the man's house. Had her celibacy caused her to lose brain cells? She definitely ought to have listened to Wendy more. Wendy!

Kate glanced at the clock. Well, she'd just go next door, lend Tyler Nichols her stuff, make some excuse to leave. After all, she'd been expecting an elderly neighbor with a potbelly, the standard on Dogwood Lane. Would she have offered to clean for him? Not by a long shot. So why should she do it because Tyler Nichols was sexy? He probably had a harem to do his bidding.

The reality was that Tyler wouldn't pay much attention to her after she helped him. He'd probably be out of the country somewhere, or with a woman who was more sophisticated than Kate was.

Which was good, Kate reminded herself. She didn't need or want to become involved with anyone at this point in her life, especially someone who lived right next door.

Kate focused. While she might have sensed a flicker of interest on his part, she'd misread signals in the past. Still, she could look, right? Looking was harmless. And Tyler Nichols was definitely eye-catching. Maybe she needed to borrow one of Nora's many pairs of binoculars. Maybe she should partake in a night of unbridled lust the way Wendy had suggested.

Tyler Nichols was probably phenomenal in bed.

Kate closed her eyes for a moment, letting her imagination take her away. He would lave her breasts, kiss her lower and lower, bring her to heights never imagined. He'd never call her a cold fish as Jack had—Jeckyll shifted in her arms and Kate's eyes flew open.

She couldn't do it. Just going to bed with someone you only lusted for seemed cold-blooded, if not plain dumb.

Deep down, Kate wanted commitment, not a quick roll in the hay—her mother's norm. Despite his good looks, which tingled her toes, she determined to steer clear of Tyler after she gave him her cleaning supplies.

As Kate put down Jeckyll, she noticed her gaping blouse and the paw prints. Embarrassment heated her face. She'd already exposed and rattled herself enough, she decided.

Sighing, she went and changed clothes, then grabbed her cleaning supplies. A knock sounded, and Kate placed the container with the supplies on the counter and threw open the door.

"Haven't I told you never to do that?" a familiar voice chided.

Not waiting for an invitation, the four-foot, ten-inch presence who dominated Dogwood Lane ushered herself in. Her snow-white hair still styled as it had been for the past twenty years, Nora waved some envelopes under Kate's nose. "You really need to check the window first. I could have been anyone. A mugger. A rapist. A murderer."

Kate sighed once more. She knew the entire spiel by heart. Hadn't she just thought it earlier, when she'd first seen Tyler at her door? "Nora, there hasn't been any crime in this neighborhood in decades, as you like to brag. You foiled the last one."

"Well, I'd hate for another crime spree to start with you. I noticed you didn't get your mail, so I grabbed it as I came over. You shouldn't leave it in your box. Might get stolen. I told you that Forrest hates to put mail in a full box, which yours would have been tomorrow. And don't forget, as of tomorrow, everyone on the block needs to have his or her Christmas lights up. It's tradition."

Kate clenched a hand behind her back and mentally

counted to ten. "The new neighbor's name is Tyler Nichols."

"Who, dear?" Nora acted as if she hadn't heard, but Kate knew better.

"Tyler Nichols. The man who moved in next door. The man over here earlier. His name is Tyler Nichols."

"Oh." Nora paused so she didn't appear too curious behind her cat-eye frames. "I wondered who was at your door. Didn't think it was a service call. Service people don't drive gas-guzzling Hummers or work this late. Did he tell you what he does for a living, dear? Is he a photojournalist as the rumormongers say?"

Patience was a virtue, Kate reminded herself and she counted to ten again. Having grown up around Nora, Kate had long ago learned to handle her, especially now that Kate was an adult. "As a matter of fact he did and he is."

Nora's gaze landed on the bucket of supplies. "I thought you cleaned on Saturdays."

Busted. Kate's shoulders slumped. Nora never missed anything. "I volunteered to help him out for a few minutes. The Dorhacks didn't do any cleaning and the place is a mess."

"Those Dorhack kids always were good-for-nothings. Poor Myra to have raised a brood like that. Not like you. You are always such a dear, especially volunteering the way you are. Sandra would be so proud."

"Thank you," Kate said as she somehow ushered Nora to the side door. But the maven wasn't to be moved outside yet.

"Since he's finally here, why I don't go home and see what I've got in the freezer? I bet the poor man hasn't had a home-cooked meal in ages. I believe I have a beef stew I can thaw out and feed him. Tell him I'll be over after I get it heated."

Kate admitted she was impressed. Nora had found a way to satisfy her curiosity and act as chaperone. She grabbed the cleaning supplies. "I'll tell him. He'll love a home-cooked meal, I'm sure." Even if he didn't, there would be no stopping it from arriving now.

"Don't forget to lock up, even though you're just going next door," Nora advised as she moved out from under Kate's carport. "Can't be too safe, you know."

"Yes, I know." Kate put her bucket on the ground and turned the key in the lock as Nora bustled across the street.

"I take it that was Nora."

Kate jumped and took a step backward. The key fell to the ground with a clink. "You scared me."

"Sorry." Tyler's grin was easy and charming, and Kate swallowed. *Could his T-shirt be any tighter?* The faded black CNN T-shirt molded to his chest and his blue jeans emphasized— Kate jolted. She did not need to be eyeing him *there*. "Let me just grab the supplies and retrieve my key."

"I'll carry them." Tyler was already beside her, bending over into her space.

"Really, it's okay." As Kate leaned to grab the supplies, her fingers collided with Tyler's. She wobbled as she straightened, clutching the bucket like a shield.

Tyler winked at her. "Let me be a chauvinist for a bit." He reached forward, and Kate simply let him pry her fingers from the carryall. She grabbed her key as Tyler started toward his place.

Having been in the house before, Kate knew that the layout mirrored hers, with a living room, eat-in kitchen, two bedrooms and a bathroom. Tyler's house also had a small addition off the kitchen—a ten-by-twelve room that could serve as a den.

"I've decided that I like it." Tyler answered Kate's unspoken question as he gave her a quick tour so she could assess the extent of the cleaning. The house wasn't in as terrible shape as he'd depicted, but as nothing had been vacuumed or scrubbed down, there was a lot of cleaning required before it met habitable standards.

They returned to the kitchen. She noticed his cabinets had been replaced with a basic oak version. Still, they and the linoleum appeared at least five years old. "So you bought this place without seeing it?" she asked.

"My twin sister picked it out after my accountant told me I needed more tax deductions and a long-term investment. I guess I could have bought something bigger, but there's no point. I'm always gone. I've heard this street has excellent resale value."

"It does," Kate said.

He opened the ancient refrigerator and pulled out a beer. "Want one?"

"No." Kate watched as Tyler removed the metal cap, tipped up the brown bottle and took a long swallow. He licked his lips. "Haven't had cold beer from my own fridge in a while. That's good. Sure you don't want one?"

"Yes." Beer might muddle her head. Already, like a sense of déjà vu that she couldn't place, she knew she'd now forgotten something important related to the beverage. Tyler moved closer and set the half-empty bottle on the counter. For some reason the man disturbed her equilibrium, and she rummaged through the cleaning supplies to maintain her composure.

"So you're always traveling," she said to keep awkward silence at bay.

"Always. I love it," he said.

"Really? All of it?"

He shook his head. "No, of course not. It's rough-and-tumble. For instance, showers are a luxury, and even having cold water is a blessing after you've been bathing with wet wipes for a few weeks. My job makes me appreciate long, hot showers, the kind you stand under until the hot water runs out."

An image of Tyler in the shower popped into Kate's head and she inhaled to clear her mind.

"But it's worth it," he continued as she tried to focus. "Ever since I took a photography class in high school, I've been hooked on telling stories through visuals. My parents bought me my first 35-millimeter camera, I went to college, interned with the local paper one summer and, to make a long story short, I got lucky and found my dream job, one that involves traveling just about everywhere. What do you do?"

Kate unloaded the cleaning supplies, deciding to stay only until Nora arrived. After all, it wasn't as though she'd be needed. As she observed him standing in his kitchen, beer bottle loose between his fingers, tight jeans and all, one fact was crystal clear. Tyler's life goals had literally fallen in his lap.

None of hers had, and her job paled in comparison. "I work for an attorney. I'm going to be a lawyer. Night school. I'll graduate in the spring. Let's get you started cleaning, because if you overheard Nora, then you know she's bringing dinner over. And, if I know Nora, you'll have a houseful of other neighbors following hard on her heels to give you the big once-over."

"Then I hope I pass their inspection." Tyler's gaze held hers for a moment, and Kate felt a tiny unrest run through her. She glanced away. There was no doubt about it. He would definitely pass. Everything about this man was sexy, strong and powerful. He even smelled good, and his voice had that deep, husky quality that sent shivers down women's spines. Like hers.

The matrons of Dogwood Lane were going to love him.

"They'll be parading their granddaughters in front of your nose in no time," Kate said as she attempted to shake off the effect he was having on her. "Be forewarned. They're all hopelessly romantic matchmakers. Nora considers herself an expert. She and Frieda are legendary."

Tyler's chuckle washed over Kate. "You sound like they've been on your case."

"All the time. They're a regular love connection," Kate admitted before adding hastily, "but I'm too busy with law school to date anyone."

"Well, I'm too busy with work," Tyler replied, grabbing the foaming spray cleaner she held out. Kate tossed a pair of yellow gloves at him and he caught them easily. "It's all-consuming and my number-one priority. Not many women want to camp out in a war zone, and there's no way I plan to settle down any time soon. Owning a house is almost too domestic for me. Especially cleaning it. You don't know of a reliable housekeeping service around here, do you?"

"No," Kate said. To her, a service would be a luxury, not a necessity.

"I'll ask around tonight." Tyler placed the gloves on the counter before shaking the aerosol can. He pressed the nozzle and foam sprayed all over the laminate countertop, the bubbles flowing over the edge onto the floor. "Darn. That didn't work."

"Haven't you ever cleaned?" Kate asked, watching as he stopped the steady stream with a rag.

He appeared sheepish. "No. I'm never around. Ever since I graduated college, I've used a service. It's a priority in my budget. If not, my place would never get clean. I like to arrive home and find everything pristine."

Just another difference between them. Kate mopped her own floors and scrubbed her own toilet every Saturday morning.

"Here, let me do that." Kate handed him a dust cloth and furniture polish. Their fingertips touched again and she pulled her hand to safety and pointed. "Why don't you go dust off the furniture? That's a no-brainer."

His eyebrow arched. "Are you saying I have no brains?"

"In this area, yes," Kate said. "You're pretty pathetic."

"You're probably right," Tyler said, laughing at her accurate assessment. "So from here on out, I'll take my orders from you."

The cheeky expression accompanying his words could thaw an iceberg, and his flirtatiousness did more than melt Kate. Longing, tingling, the sudden need for raw passion hit her. Men like Tyler Nichols were dangerous. They stole your heart and gave you nothing but lingering memories. That is, if you even got to that point at all. She had to get away from him. Kate gestured toward the living room. "Dust!"

"Yes, ma'am," Tyler said and disappeared through the archway, leaving Kate alone to deal with her yearnings and wipe up the mess.

Chapter Three

A little less than two hours later, Tyler Nichols decided he had it made. His new neighbors were on a mission, and, after telling Tyler to sit and enjoy some of Nora's homemade stew, they had flown into a cleaning frenzy while clucking nonstop about Myra's dreadful children.

Even if Tyler had wanted to help, sitting at the kitchen table was probably safer. The Dogwood matrons were household pros who put Heloise and her hints to shame.

They were also matchmakers extraordinaire who had to be reckoned with. Subtlety was not in the vocabulary of these ladies. Tyler had already gracefully turned down three invitations to meet six eligible granddaughters.

Not only that, but the few men who had braved coming into the fray were busy one-upping one another to carry any remaining boxes. No, Tyler decided that sitting was safer, and better because it allowed him to look at Kate as she moved around, spritzing and polishing.

Even doing something as mundane as household chores revealed the feminine grace basic to her. That type of poise was rare and would make her fun to photograph.

Her face had all the planes and angles the camera

lens loved. He only wished she'd pull her hair out of that annoying bun. With her hair around her shoulders, she would laugh, bat her long eyelashes and gesture him toward the bedroom.... Tyler shook off the vision before it threw him completely off balance. Once his shower was suitably sanitized, he was heading in there for a needed dose of cold water.

To think of Kate simply as his next-door neighbor would be wise, he reminded himself. Whereas he loved the female sex, and he most definitely enjoyed their company as long as it came without strings, he was not one of those men who knew the meaning of the C-word. The only commitment he'd made was to his career. He'd never remained with one woman long enough even to think about giving her a key to his apartment or allowing her to store a toothbrush there.

But after a grandma named Frieda had cornered him and suggested that he ask Kate out, well, now the idea wouldn't dislodge itself. Her body between his sheets— just the very idea was a muse beckoning.

Tyler twisted his hands. Maybe Kate was right about declaring him brainless. Here he was, considering following Frieda's suggestion. While he didn't know Kate well, he sensed she could prove to be a disastrous complication in his life. And when the relationship ended, he'd still be living next door to her. How awkward would that be?

He knew only one other woman like Kate. His mother. Efficient. Sweet. Innocent. Always lending a helping hand. Definitely untarnished by the ugliness of the world. Maybe that was why his mom didn't understand his job and wanted him settled down, not traveling the world as he preferred.

Not even his job's importance could convince his mother to like his decision to be free to document the world's events on film. Not that she had given up on seeing him married. She remained hopeful that if Tyler found the right woman, he'd want to stay home.

Somehow, Tyler didn't figure Kate would really understand the value of his job, either. The way she fit into the Dogwood Lane community proved she was home and hearth, something he definitely was not and never would be.

"Earth to Tyler!"

Tyler jerked his head up to find Kate hovering over him. Her breasts were just about eye level, and Tyler shoved his hands under his legs.

"Are you just going to sit there, or are you going to unpack? Didn't you hear me? They've finished your bedroom and Harold wants to know if you're happy with where the movers put the furniture. If you are, you'd better hurry in there before they decide to rearrange it and move it around themselves."

Tyler gave a short laugh before standing up and stretching. "I'd better go survey the scene."

"You'd better. I've never seen so many men trying to play Hercules."

As Kate smiled, Tyler's gut clenched. He attempted to put the evening into proper perspective. "By the way, in case I forget to tell you later, thanks for organizing this."

"No problem," she said.

"No, really," Tyler insisted. He gestured around. "I'll have to tell my sister I lucked out. She's the one who picked out this house. I'm glad I listened to her. You guys are great."

Kate stepped away and vigorously wiped the counter,

the same one she had scoured earlier. "Well," she said, refusing to look at him, "consider it your housewarming present from all of us. Dogwood Lane is a pretty special place. We're more than a street. We're a neighborhood."

"I'd definitely say so." Tyler couldn't resist. He rose and approached her. His fingers snaked forward and tugged on the infernal bun that was driving him crazy. Blondish strands cascaded to her shoulders and her head shot up. She stood as if hypnotized, watching him, waiting for his next move. His nose wrinkled. Even with a hint of antiseptic woodsy pine, she still smelled divine.

Tyler inwardly cursed himself. Yep, way too long without a woman. That had to be the reason he was having this overwhelming reaction to Kate. He'd better move away before he did something stupid and impulsive, like kiss those lips, which were slightly parted with anticipation. "Those guys are waiting."

"Yes." Her voice faltered as she moved a pace back. "Good idea."

As soon as he left the room, Kate sat in the chair he had vacated. The wood still felt warm from his presence.

Wow. Whenever he'd touched her, even briefly, she'd felt shivers run down to her toes. Jack had never made her quiver. Certainly not like this. Tyler had boldly pulled her hair from her bun. Forgetting she had gloves on, she reached up to touch the strands.

"He's quite a doll, don't you think?" Frieda strode into the room, a small white trash bag dangling from her hand. "I tell you, if I were forty years younger, he wouldn't stand a chance."

"He's very nice," Kate hedged. There was no way to describe what Tyler was, but *doll* didn't come close. He put Barbie's ex, Ken, to shame.

"He's definitely an improvement over Myra, God bless her. We could use some younger blood on the street."

"Are you matchmaking again?" Nora entered and glared at Frieda.

Frieda didn't hide her guilt. "Of course I am. I think Tyler would be a good match for anyone."

"He's busy with work, as am I," Kate replied, deciding to nip this situation in the bud. All night Frieda and Nora had swept her along, and she couldn't escape the feeling she'd forgotten something important.

Besides, she'd had enough of Frieda's and Nora's matchmaking attempts two years ago after Sandra's death. To prove to the matrons she wasn't hurting anymore, Kate had gone on three disastrous blind dates, and then she'd rebounded straight into Jack. There were worse things than being alone, she reminded herself.

Nora patted Kate on the shoulder. "There, there, dear. Ignore Frieda. Niles will be in town over Christmas. That's only a few weeks away."

Great. Kate sighed inwardly. She had no intention of dating Niles, either. She just didn't have the heart to tell Nora outright, which she'd have to do if Nora kept insisting on fixing them up. Nora had been such a support after Sandra's death that Kate hated to flat-out reject her grandson. Thus, getting out of a date would take some creative thought. "I'm busy with school and work," she said somewhat lamely.

Nora didn't seem too perturbed. "We'll just have to arrange something that fits into your schedule. You'll love Niles. He was a magna cum laude at Georgia Tech."

"He's a geek," Frieda announced. "You can say no, Kate. Have you seen Niles's photos?"

"Frieda Webster!" Nora placed her aged hands on her hips and gazed over her glasses. Despite her petite size, Nora packed a powerful punch. "You take that back. Niles is perfect for Kate."

Frieda tossed her head, her hair-sprayed gray hair not budging an inch. "No, he's not. Tyler's much better."

"Much better at what?" Tyler strode back into the room and grinned. "Thelma—I think that's her name— is organizing my underwear drawer. I figured a hasty retreat was best."

Still sitting in the chair, Kate dropped her head into her hands. How could he be so nonchalant and naive? Didn't he have a clue? Dogwood Lane would be gossiping about his boxers or briefs for weeks to come. The residents thrived on things like that to spice up their bunco nights.

"Well," Nora said, relaxing her posture somewhat, "why don't you just take a break and keep us company. I was telling Kate all about my grandson Niles. He's visiting over the holidays. Normally, I travel to Jacksonville, but this year, as the family is going every which way, he's agreed to come down here for a change."

"Really?" Tyler feigned interest as he poured himself a glass of water from the tap. He'd given up on beer after finishing the first one.

"Yes. Did Rita tell you about her granddaughter Jane? Such a pretty little thing. She's an elementary teacher in Lakeland."

Tyler shrugged. "She forgot to mention that part."

"Well, you'll have to meet her. Just like Kate is going to meet my Niles," Nora declared.

"Oh, I'm sure she's looking forward to it," Tyler said, giving Kate a wink. After listening to all the single-women stories, he knew exactly what Kate dealt with. Her neighbors were the matchmakers from hell.

"Of course Kate wants to meet Niles," Nora insisted.

Frieda coughed, the noise sounding like the word *bull*.

"Frieda!" Nora's expression was aghast.

"Something stuck in my throat," Frieda said, waving her hand in front of her face.

"I'm going to check on Thelma." As if unable to endure the conversation any longer, Kate left the room.

"So. About Jane," Nora began, ignoring Kate's departure.

"About Jane," Tyler interrupted. He had no plans to date anyone's granddaughter. Although Kate… She was someone he wouldn't mind knowing better—intimately better—in spite of his rule not to get involved with his neighbors.

"It's probably just as well that I don't meet Jane," Tyler said, ready to stop the matchmaking madness. "Unfortunately, I don't have time for relationships. I'll be on another assignment in just a few days. While I'm thinking of it, my sister is a tall thin blonde who drives a BMW convertible. Tara will pop by occasionally when I'm out of town to check on the place. She's got a key."

Nora nodded. "I'm glad you told me. We're very careful on this street."

"She keeps binoculars and a notebook by every window," Frieda said.

Good grief. He'd thought Kate had been exaggerating. "Kate said you were very vigilant."

"Someone has to be. There's nowhere safe anymore," Nora said. "Have you ever seen those *It Takes a Thief* shows?"

"The last bit of action we had on this block was when raccoons knocked over Elmer's trash cans last year," Frieda interjected.

"One still can't be too careful," Nora persisted, shooting Frieda a dirty look. "Kate is prone to just opening her door without peering outside first. And you can't leave windows ajar anymore without having window guards. My Niles is good with tools. He said he'd install some for Kate while he's here."

Niles in Kate's house? Even though he'd known Kate mere hours, Tyler didn't like the sound of that. "You know, Nora, the fact that this neighborhood is pretty safe is a credit to you, and I can agree with your point. I'll secure Kate's windows. I'm quite handy, although probably not as handy as your Niles."

That sounded good. Compliment and go for what you want at the same time. His mama hadn't raised a fool.

"You'd do that?" Nora paused, her expression skeptical behind her glasses.

"Of course I would. I could also get it done sooner, since security is of such essence and Niles won't be here for a few weeks. The TV news just reported on how thieves increase their activity around the holidays."

He wasn't sure if that was true, and he drew himself up a little straighter under Nora's scrutiny. "After all," he told her, "it's the very least I can do after Kate's been so neighborly to help me out by cleaning."

"Hmm." Nora pondered the idea for a moment, refusing to cave easily.

"I think you should take her to dinner, instead," Frieda stated. Her smile widened. "In fact, that would be a perfect way to repay Kate for her generosity tonight. In addition to fixing her windows, of course."

"Really, that's not necessary," Nora declared, shooting Frieda a signal Tyler couldn't quite decipher.

"Dinner," Frieda insisted, cutting Nora off. "How about that idea, Tyler?"

In for a penny...

"I think dinner might just be doable."

FROM HER VANTAGE POINT outside the doorway, Kate saw Tyler's nod of agreement. Instantly, her heart dropped like a stone.

Did the man not have a clue? Of course not. Tyler was a man—meaning, he was dense. He'd just moved in, but it didn't take a rocket scientist to realize what everyone else knew—that Frieda and Nora wanted Kate married, and Frieda would be happier if it wasn't to Nora's nerdy grandson, Niles.

Best friends for over thirty years, Nora and Frieda were also each other's worst enemies, especially when matchmaking and gin games were involved. Each of them hated when the other one won. Ever since Sandra had died, the two women had taken on Kate's love life as a top priority, second only to those gin games and the Neighborhood Watch.

Ready to put an end to the dinner idea, Kate stepped into the kitchen. However, the daring look Tyler shot her curled her toes, and Kate struggled for composure. Did she wipe that smug expression off his face by rejecting his offer, or take his challenge and accept?

Tyler Nichols had the body of a god. From what she'd seen of his interaction with the Dogwood Lane matrons, he also had a sense of humor. His job told Kate that he had bravery, drive and ambition. He could afford a decent house. He was the type of man she could fall for.

But his career meant he wouldn't stick around. Kate needed permanence.

Best to remain simply neighbors. Look, but don't touch. Dream, but don't dare. Be safe. The fantasy was always better than the reality. The heck with not appearing weak. Bowing out gracefully was the better option. Pandora's box would remain closed.

"Take her somewhere good," Frieda told Tyler. "Kate doesn't get out enough, and her idea of eating out is fast food."

"That's for sure," Nora added, stealing the conversation. "I can't even convince her to slow down long enough to go to Ponderosa with me."

Tyler arched his eyebrows and peered down his nose at Kate. Defiance sparkled in his warm chocolate eyes as he prepared for her rejection.

"How about I take her to a wonderful little microbrewery I know of, Nora?" Tyler proposed. "The food is the best, and they brew their beer on the spot. It's also off the beaten tourist path…on the other side of town, over by where I used to live."

"Kate doesn't like beer." Nora gave a sniff.

Kate bristled. How did Nora know what Kate did and didn't like? Time to regain control of this situation, especially since it was *her* life they were planning. She shouldn't have let the silliness go on this long, as it was. "Would you three stop talking about me like I'm not here?"

She drew herself up and moved to stand near them. "For your information, Nora, I've been known to have an occasional beer. I just don't prefer it, that's all. A microbrewery sounds like fun. Although I'm really not available. I work full-time and I have school, remember? Finals start next week and I have a major research paper due."

"Fine." Frieda gave a huff that was all for show. "I was only trying to be helpful. You need to socialize more. You're always cooped up in that house."

Kate rubbed her hands on her sweatpants. Wendy had pretty well said the same thing. "I'm sure Tyler and I can find a time convenient to both of us to have dinner—*if* we decide to go to dinner." She stressed the *if,* hoping Tyler would catch on. "No help from either of you is necessary."

"Tomorrow night," Tyler said. "How about it, Kate?"

Had he not heard her say *if?* Frustration found her, and Kate began formulating her excuse. But in the midst of delivering her refusal, she paused. Neither Frieda nor Nora was paying any attention to her. Instead, Nora was peering through Tyler's blinds. "Someone just pulled into your driveway, Kate. Driving a dark blue sports car."

Kate glanced at the clock on the stove. She'd set the time herself. Eight-fifteen. That meant... Oh no! Once Nora had arrived, she'd only meant to stay a few minutes. Had that much time really elapsed? How could she have forgotten? Then again, how could she have missed the Hummer? Today was simply not her day....

Chapter Four

As Kate threw her hands up in exasperation, for the second time that day Tyler caught himself staring at her chest. Droplets of water from the yellow gloves had adhered to her shirt and formed an interesting pattern that his fingers suddenly itched to touch.

Kate began peeling off the gloves. "I forgot all about Wendy. She's going to kill me. I'm not ready for the party!"

"You're going to a party?" Those gray eyebrows of Nora's lifted in query. "You never go to parties."

"I go to parties," Kate protested. "Not often, but I go. And I was attending this one. I was supposed to be ready at eight. I only planned on being over here a little while."

"It's a quarter after," Nora replied with a shrug, as if it were somehow Wendy's fault. "She's late."

Kate dropped the gloves in Tyler's sink. "She'll never forgive me for forgetting that we had plans. We talked before she left the office."

"Why don't I go over to your place with you?" Tyler offered. "I'll explain that I sidetracked you."

"Thanks, but that won't help," Kate said. She paused a moment. "Seriously, I'm not trying to be rude. It's a sweet thought, but no matter what, Wendy will be furious with me when she discovers I'm not ready. I promised. I'll have to meet her at the party. I still need a shower, and— Oh!"

Tyler had gripped her elbow, and Kate was looking up at him in surprise. Ah, immediate silence. So the technique did work. Tyler had often seen his father merely put his hand on his mother's arm, and instantly, she'd stop speaking, even in midsentence. Kate's expression was not one of passivity but of interest. Again her lips were parted, and her mouth was delectable open like that. Definitely kissable.

Tyler continued to hold Kate's elbow, and her skin warmed where his fingers curled around her arm. Interesting. He decided he liked touching her and made a mental note to continue exploring the phenomenon of touching Kate.

"I told you I would come with you," he told her. "Let's go meet this Wendy friend of yours."

Tyler threw open the door without looking first, the movement receiving Nora's reproach. He ignored her disapproval. If bullets flying over his head counted, he had definitely been in many more dangerous situations than this one.

"Wendy?" Kate called.

"Kate! Are you outside?" Wendy stood under Kate's carport, her hand over her eyes as she squinted into the shadows. Normally, Tyler appreciated tall leggy brunettes, but none had affected his equilibrium quite like the shorter blond woman by his side.

"Ah, you must be Wendy," Tyler said as he and Kate stepped into the light.

"Kate!" Wendy shrieked as she saw Kate's attire. "You're not ready! You forgot!" And then, as if realization dawned, Wendy's gaze registered that Tyler stood there. Her mouth opened into a silent O.

"Hi, Wendy. I'm Tyler." He held out his hand, and Wendy returned his firm grasp with a limp handshake. "Kate was just telling me about you. It's true she only now remembered your party. I'm afraid I've been distracting her terribly. I just moved in today and—"

Tyler broke off as Kate's jaw dropped open as though to say something. Tyler put a forefinger under her chin, leaned over and whispered in her ear, "Shut your mouth, darling. I might have to do something to help you shut it."

Wendy's mouth closed at the same time as Kate's, Tyler noted with a grin. Oh, how he loved American women. They were the greatest in the world, and not just because they were so predictable. He knew exactly what thought had crossed each of their minds at his deliberate words. He gave Wendy a devilish smile.

"Wendy, please don't blame Kate," Tyler continued. "She didn't mean to lose track of time. These things sort of happen. She did tell me she could be ready quickly. She needs to grab a shower first."

Wendy wobbled on her high heels as she eased toward her car. "You could have called, Kate, and let me know about your change of plans."

Kate found her voice. "Wendy! It's not like this. We just met. He and I aren't— I mean, we're only neighbors. He lives right there."

Kate attempted to squirm away from Tyler, but he tugged her wiggling body closer and pressed her to him. She fit nicely against his hip, and a current passed between them, sending warmth even lower. To hide his immediate arousal, Tyler drew Kate tighter.

Damn, she felt good. Despite his obvious physical state, Kate didn't even attempt to pull away but instead seemed almost to sink into his skin, as if she belonged there.

"It's okay." Tyler purposely made his tone soothing. She was going to kill him later, but it was a small price to pay. Kate's body touching his was sending sensual signals to his brain unlike any he'd ever experienced. Being a red-blooded male, he was enjoying every one. "Wendy's a grown woman who knows how these things happen. Right, Wendy?"

Wendy nodded as she inched backward and Tyler turned his attention to Kate. "Are you with Wendy or with me? If you're staying with me, there's still some work to finish in my bedroom."

"I—" Kate began.

"We'll talk Monday," Wendy called as she passed the bumper of Kate's car. Then, without waiting for Kate's answer, Wendy jumped into her vehicle and drove away.

Once the taillights disappeared, Kate jerked herself out of Tyler's embrace. Her fists rose as if to pummel him. Her body shook. Was she…crying?

Remorse immediately overtook Tyler. Was he destined to be an insensitive cad? While it was the truth, he had greatly stretched the situation out of proportion, letting Wendy think the worst. The last thing he wanted was his new neighbor to think that he was some sort of caveman. "Kate, I'm sorry. I didn't mean to…"

Then he noticed the small upturn of her full lips, next her straight white teeth. She was smiling, laughing even, so hard that tears were beginning to run down her cheeks.

"I can't believe it. Did you notice her expression?

Wendy probably assumes I'm sleeping with you. You! She thinks I... We... As if..." Kate's words dissolved into more laughter and she doubled over, holding her stomach.

Confused, Tyler tossed his arms out in a gesture of "Excuse me?" What was going on with her? He knew women liked him. He'd even been told he was a good lover. But Kate, with her cute giggle, had deflated the ego his sister had always claimed was oversize to start with. Maybe coming outside with her hadn't been a good idea. Maybe he should have let her handle her problem herself. She obviously didn't need him. And he had been pretty overboard.

"This'll be all over the office by Monday morning," Kate explained as Tyler struggled to assess the depth of his mistake. "All over the grapevine. I should be killing you because this is so embarrassing. Still, I'm laughing because it's the opposite of the truth. As if me... you. I love it."

Tyler felt wounded. So much for saving damsels in distress. In return, they trashed your pride. He coughed. "Look, Kate, do you want to go to the party? You can still meet Wendy there. I've got everything under control here and—"

Kate interrupted him with another giggle. "Oh, no. Now that I think about it, this is much better. Thank you."

"You're thanking me? I thought I'd just embarrassed you." Tyler frowned. Confusion was not a state he found himself in very often. He wasn't sure that he liked that he could negotiate tiny rebel countries and mercenaries with AK–47s better than he could figure out Kate Merrill.

Kate's loose hair danced around her shoulders as she nodded. "Oh, yes. It's perfect. Don't you see?"

Tyler crossed his arms. "No. I'm in the dark. Please enlighten me."

Another giggle. Her laughter should have been infectious, but he wasn't amused.

"Tyler, you've recharged the office gossip for months. I work with Wendy, so she'll share the news. If all my coworkers think we're having a torrid affair, then they'll stop trying to fix me up with every Tom, Dick and Harry and leave me in peace."

"And you want that?" Tyler's stomach rumbled. Maybe Nora's stew wasn't sitting well.

"Oh, I want it, all right. Just because I'm twenty-seven doesn't mean I'm over the hill. I'm sick of people thinking that just because I don't have a man in my life something's wrong with me. Now everyone at the office will believe I'm dating you and they'll stop harping on me to…"

She paused, and he swore that even in the carport light he saw her blush. "Well, they'll stop. No one will be the wiser, and since you'll never be home, we'll never see each other, either. It's perfect."

Tyler frowned. Perhaps she'd inhaled too many cleaning fumes while working on his house. "Perfect?"

"Oh, yes. This is the perfect way to repay me. No need for us to go on a real date. I mean, Wendy met you, so no one will be the wiser. Yes, it's perfect."

Really. For whom? Earlier he'd thought about asking her out. He'd even thought about kissing those perfect lips. He'd taken her hair out of its bun. Hell, he was attracted to her. So how had he become her fake date, and the one she'd use to keep the matchmakers at bay?

In less than a minute, she'd made him into a ghost. He didn't like it. Not one bit.

"Are you two going to remain there all night, or are you coming back inside?" Nora waited, silhouetted in the doorway to Tyler's kitchen. "We're just about finished, and we want to make sure you're happy before we get our beauty sleep. We aren't getting any younger, you know."

"On our way," Kate called.

As they walked toward his house, Tyler wondered exactly how much Nora had heard. He decided to worry about that later. Tonight he'd sleep in his own bed, in his own house. He could use a good night's rest to help him deal with the situation called Kate.

Abruptly, he stopped. "Five o'clock tomorrow."

Kate paused on the doorstep. "Tyler, you don't have to take me out. Frieda was just talking. Didn't we already reach an understanding out in the carport? We don't have to go on an actual date."

"Five o'clock. That way we can do dinner and a movie. Maybe drive through one of those Christmas-light displays."

There must have been something in his tone that convinced her, for she said, "Okay."

"Great. It's a date." He hesitated a fraction of a second before following her into his kitchen. Fake date. Ghost. He'd see about that.

THE NEXT DAY Tyler awoke to glorious silence. No beeping of a battery-powered watch alarm. No buzzing insects. No gunfire or bloodcurdling screams. Instead, sunlight filtered through newly dusted blinds. His bed was soft, his pillow comfortable. He rolled over, unwilling to move from his little slice of heaven. Finally, he glanced at the clock. Noon. He'd slept almost twelve hours.

He threw his arms over his head and stretched. Nothing like a good night's sleep to soothe the aches of the mind, body and soul. Outside, a bird chirped. Then another. He closed his eyes and listened for a moment. He didn't know anything about birds, so he couldn't tell what species they were, but it didn't matter. Eyes still closed, Tyler simply enjoyed their warbling. In war-torn countries, birdsong simply didn't exist.

Singing?

Tyler sat up in bed, the crisp white sheet slipping to his waist. He reached over and parted the blinds. *Kate* was singing.

She stood next to the chain-link fence separating their backyards. In one hand she held a trowel and in the other she held a green plastic bucket, the type usually used for holding soapy water. Kate bent, dug up some dead brown thing and then dropped it into her bucket. And all the while she was singing. Broadway musicals, Tyler noted. She was running through renditions of the famous ones, even songs she knew only part of the verses to.

Tyler smiled. Peeping Tom he wasn't, but he still had to stare. His new neighbor didn't have a clue how sexy she was. She wore hot-pink gardening gloves, a big straw, brimmed hat, blue jeans that emphasized a nice rounded bottom and a tight red T-shirt that she filled out quite nicely.

Dig, flick, move.

He watched her for one extra moment, struck by her grace and beauty. Kate intrigued him. How he was going to make anything work between them he didn't know, but for some reason, it was as essential as breathing that he explore the sensations he experienced every time he was around her.

Tyler let the blinds snap closed, threw his legs over the edge of his bed and padded to the bathroom. Unlike the fickle cold showers he'd become accustomed to as a war correspondent, warm water gushed from the pipes and pounded his tight muscles. Reluctant to leave, Tyler relaxed under the heavy spray longer than necessary. By twelve-thirty he'd finished his coffee and toast. The view out his kitchen window revealed Kate still digging and flipping.

He watched her once more, thinking that there was something innate in her that put glamorous women to shame. Maybe if he photographed her, he could tell what it was. Photos often captured what the human eye missed. Maybe studying her still image could help him figure out why she fascinated him.

Tyler put his dishes in the sink before checking his pager and cell phone. Both had been wondrously silent. Not that he'd really expected his sister to call him back. The surprise, though, was that his assignment editor hadn't contacted him yet. Maybe Jess really was serious about giving him a well-deserved break until after the new year. He shook his head, sending shaggy brown hair over one eye. Nah. He'd bet Jess would only give him until tomorrow before she called with his next assignment specifics. He'd requested stateside so he could stay in Orlando for the holidays. That would make his mom happy. He'd missed last year's family festivities and his mom hadn't been too pleased.

His aluminum screen door squeaked when he opened

it, and Kate's head popped up at the sound. Tyler kept his whistle of appreciation under his breath as she stood. "Hi."

"Hey," Kate replied. She wiped her forehead with the back of her gloved hand. The movement left a smudge of dirt on her face. With her pigtails, floppy hat and dirt-smudged face, she looked ready to step into Becky Thatcher's shoes and follow Tom Sawyer anywhere. Not only was she sexy, she was adorable. In order to control his libido, Tyler mentally gave himself a cold shower.

"So how was your first night in your new house?" she asked.

"Awesome. I got up a little while ago. What are you doing?"

"Garden cleanup. I'm a little behind, but since it's such a nice day I thought I'd get outside and finish before I hang the rest of my Christmas lights. Underneath all these dead stalks are my live-forevers."

"Oh." Tyler nodded despite the fact he had no idea what live-forevers were.

"I love to garden. Growing up, I always swore I would never garden the way my grandmother did. I told her I wasn't going to get my fingers dirty. But once you start digging, you're hooked. Sandra was one in a million."

"Sandra was your grandmother."

"Right. She hated being called Grandmother. Said it made her feel old. So I called her Sandra. She was the one who raised me."

"What about your mom?" Tyler asked.

"She died a few years back. The guy whose car she was in was drunk. He hit a tree at ninety."

"I'm sorry," Tyler said.

Kate shrugged. "It used to bother me, but more so that I felt relieved. I mean, is that morbid? You're not supposed to feel relief, but I did. Sandra was really the only family I had. Once grade school began, she insisted I stay with her. Gosh, I shouldn't be telling you this. You'll think I'm nuts."

"No, I won't," Tyler said. "I'm a journalist. We're good listeners. We don't judge. So you grew up with everyone I met last night."

Kate didn't appear too won over by his sincerity, but she continued anyway. "Pretty much. This street has a very low turnover. You've heard that it-takes-a-village statement. Well, everyone on this block took an interest in my upbringing. I couldn't get into any trouble without Sandra hearing about it within two seconds."

"What about your dad?"

Kate's expression clouded and she gave another non-chalant shrug, as if to dismiss her feelings. "I never knew him. He died when I was a baby. Sandra was actually his aunt."

"She sounds like a wonderful person." The force of his empathy surprised him. He'd had such a terrific childhood, with two happily married parents who had always supported him in anything he did, whether they liked his choices or not. They'd been his cheerleaders, his home base and his rock. His gut reaction to Kate's description of her family was one of anger—someone as lovely as her should have had something better.

"So, what brings you by?" Kate asked, switching the topic.

"I believe we have a date. Does the microbrewery still sound okay? Afterward, I'm liking that outdoor-light-show idea more and more. I haven't been to one of those in years."

Kate smiled wistfully. "Oh, Tyler. Now that you live here, you've got to learn to smile and nod when Frieda or Nora talk. It's safer that way."

She was dismissing him and he frowned. He'd never had to persuade a woman. "Kate, you helped me clean, and if nothing else, I'd like to take you to dinner. Even if it was Frieda's idea, I make my own decisions. Always have. Always will."

"Oh." She seemed astonished by this.

He pressed on. "If I remember right, we said five. The place gets crazy after seven. That's why it's better to go early. If you'd like to do something more local, we could do that, instead. Just say so."

He waited for a moment and then played his trump card. "Besides, if you're serious about what you said last night—that is, about pretending I'm your boyfriend—you should get to know me a little. If not, that six-degrees-of-separation thing could trip you up."

Kate considered his argument for a minute, the angle of her hat hiding her expression. She inhaled a deep breath. "You're probably right. With my luck, I'd run into someone who knows you. I guess I will have to tell Wendy your name."

He nodded, warming to his persuasive argument. "Exactly. This plan of yours might backfire if you get tripped up. You'll need to have some information on me. So dinner?"

"Okay. Dinner, but I pay my way. And the microbrewery is fine. Let's keep five. Frieda asked me to drive her to church tomorrow, so I don't want to stay out late. She goes to the early service."

"That's okay." Tyler gently touched her forearm for emphasis.

He knew his mistake the moment his fingers connected with her bare skin. The sizzle was even stronger than what had passed between them the previous night. Kate even appeared shaken as he moved his fingers away. "Well, I'm off to pick up my new appliances. You should see the old ones."

"I did. Last night," Kate reminded him with a nod that bounced her dark blond pigtails. Tyler stilled his fingers, pushing aside the urge to run his hands through her hair and free the strands from the confining bands.

"Then you understand why I'm going to go get them," Tyler said.

"You're doing it yourself?"

Tyler laughed. "I've got older brothers. They work for pizza and beer, which is a lot cheaper than a delivery service."

Kate brushed a hand across her forehead, causing more dirt to fall across her nose like brown freckles. "Do you really figure you'll be back by five? You don't have a lot of time. We can always postpone. Your brothers probably haven't visited with you in ages."

"Five is fine. I know how to get them moving," Tyler said. "I'll see you later."

Kate watched him climb into his SUV and back out. She shook her head and now dirt dropped from her bangs. She was a mess, yet Tyler hadn't minded. Interesting. Jack had always been concerned about what she was wearing and how she looked. He'd wanted to change most things about her. And he had hated her garden. Speaking of… She surveyed her backyard. Only one fence length to go and then she'd start installing her Christmas lights.

TYLER COULDN'T BELIEVE it was after three-thirty. It was the darkest part of the year and he would be losing sunlight within the next hour. With a grimace he glanced at the digital clock on his dashboard.

"That's the sixth time you've checked out the clock," his brother Leo observed. "Never known a man so much in a hurry to install a dishwasher. Either you've got a sinkful of dishes, or you've got a hot date. Since you've been out of town, I'd guess the latter."

Tyler gripped the steering wheel of the Hummer a little tighter. "I have to be somewhere at five, that's all."

Leo gave a short laugh. "If you're late, it's your fault. You should've planned on Mom feeding you lunch. She hasn't seen you in what amounts to forever in her book. You know how she worries. You can go months without contact and she just has to assume that silence means everything's okay."

"Yeah, well," Tyler said as he exited the interstate. His job was like that.

"So you caved and stayed to eat. That was a wise and manly thing to do. You've always been her baby, and staying made her happy," Leo pointed out.

Tyler sighed. His mother had insisted on cooking soup and whipping up some sandwiches before she would let Tyler or his dad hook up the trailer. His parents lived forty-five minutes on the other side of Orlando via Interstate 4, and Tyler was running desperately behind schedule. Worse, a Suburban-load of his family followed to help.

How he was going to get them to install the appliances and leave quickly without being subjected to the full brunt of a Nichols family inquisition was beyond him. He'd wanted to call Kate, but Information had told him that her number was unlisted. He hadn't thought to ask her for it since he lived next door.

"So, what's she like?" Leo asked.

Tyler executed a full stop before turning onto Dogwood Lane. "What?"

"Not what. Who." Leo grinned, and Tyler suddenly wished he'd hired a delivery service. In the long run it might have been easier and faster.

"You've barely been in town for a day and you've got a date, one you're already concerned about being late for. That's not like you. This must be some babe if you're not willing to leave her waiting," Leo said.

Tyler pulled in to his driveway. "She's not some babe. She's my next-door neighbor. I promised her dinner in exchange for helping me out last night."

Leo gave a low whistle. "Boy, she must have helped something out for you to move that fast."

"Look, Leo," Tyler said, exiting the Hummer, "Kate's my neighbor. This street is big on Southern hospitality—obviously, something a cracker like you doesn't understand."

"Maybe not," Leo said, not subdued in the slightest and taking the putdown as a joke. "Hey, guys," Leo yelled as everyone piled out of the Suburban. "Tyler's got a date tonight! He's already being neighborly."

Tyler let a foul word fly as Leo went over and high-fived Jamie and Craig. Even Tyler's father, Chad, grinned. Everyone was amused at Tyler's expense. "I swear, Leo, I'll whip you yet," Tyler said, threatening to do the Southern thing of calling his brother out and beating him to a pulp. Of course, Tyler had never been able to whip Leo, but even getting in a few licks might make him feel better.

"I see you grew a big mouth overseas," Leo said with a laugh as he tugged on the dishwasher crate and loaded it onto a dolly. Already Jamie, Craig and his dad were unloading the other appliances.

Tyler unlocked the kitchen door and held it open as his brother Jamie moved the refrigerator into the house. Jamie pulled a knife out of his pocket and began to slice open the box. "At least you'll have a real refrigerator, not that ancient thing over there pretending to keep the beer cold. You do have beer, right, Tyler? I'm not doing this for nothing."

A knock at the door stopped Tyler from having to reply. "Hello? Tyler?"

Even less than twenty-four hours later, Tyler would have recognized her voice anywhere. Kate. He began to move toward the door, but because Jamie was by the utility closet, he got there first.

"Hello." Kate smiled tentatively as she stepped into the kitchen. In one hand she held a pitcher of ice-cold lemonade, complete with floating lemon slices. In the other she held a stack of plastic cups. Her dark blond hair hung loose around her shoulders, giving her the appearance of an angel. "I noticed the empty trailer, and thought y'all might be thirsty."

Jamie reached for the pitcher. "We are, ma'am. Here. Let me get that. So you must be the lovely neighbor Tyler's been telling us about."

"Oh." Kate blushed, and Tyler glared at his brother, who deliberately sent Kate his best smile. Regaining his senses, Tyler crossed the floor in two giant strides.

He took the plastic cups from her hand, his fingers lingering on hers as he did so. Her eyes widened at his touch. "This is a wonderful surprise. Thank you," he told her.

"Yeah, Tyler was just telling us about his neighbors," Leo piped up from where he was unpacking the dryer. "I'm Leo."

"He's married. I'm not," Jamie replied, setting the pitcher on the counter. He winked at Kate, and Tyler immediately clenched his hands.

"Yeah, no one would have him," Craig piped in. He saw Jamie's expression and grinned. "Too good to pass up, bro. By the way, Kate, I'm Craig. You'll learn to ignore us when we're all together."

"Boys." With one spoken word they all fell silent and turned as one to face their father. Chad waited with his arms across his chest. Suddenly, Craig studied his feet. Jamie moved a step or two away from the counter. Only Tyler stood rooted, unwilling to move too far from Kate. "How about you pour that lemonade, Jamie," his father suggested.

Kate faced Tyler. "I baked some Christmas cookies this morning, and there's no way I can eat all of them. Why don't I go get you some?"

"Wow." Jamie whistled as soon as Kate disappeared. "Aren't you the lucky one?"

"That's right." Tyler drew himself up. "Me. I'm the lucky one. And whereas I can't whip Leo, I can whip you."

Craig laughed. "I'd say Tyler's staking his claim, Jamie old boy. Seems like you're out of luck this round."

Jamie poured himself a cup of lemonade and took a long sip. "You know, Tyler, if her cookies are as good as this lemonade, you don't deserve her. I'm the steady hometown one who's ready to settle down now that I'm thirty-five. You're always off somewhere. A woman like her won't put up with that nonsense for long. She deserves much more, something better than you."

Tyler didn't want to think about his brother's remarks. He recognized that Kate was home and hearth through and through; he just hadn't figured out how to reconcile his world-traveling career and the girl next door. But as certain as the sun was setting, Tyler wanted to explore the sensations he'd felt only with Kate.

Now if only he could get his family out of his house so he could get started on his date. He glanced around. Having hooked up the dryer hose, Leo was maneuvering the appliance into place. His father and Craig were installing the washing machine, and the new refrigerator was now humming, although the old one still sat in the middle of the room. They really didn't have much more work to do. Then Tyler heard a crunch of gravel and he winced. So much for ditching his family. Reinforcements in the form of his mother and Leo's wife, Ellen, had just arrived.

Not good. While he loved his family, tonight he'd hoped to get to know Kate. The next assignment and *poof*, maybe these sensations he had with Kate would have vanished by the time he returned.

Normally, Tyler wouldn't care. Any other woman and he'd risk it. But with Kate, he didn't want to miss this chance.

Chapter Five

Kate picked up the Christmas cookies, and as she placed her hand on the doorknob, she paused. What was she doing bringing the man cookies? She'd already brought him a pitcher of ice-cold lemonade.

She winced and turned around, ready to return the plate to the counter. The cookie giving smacked of more than neighborly interest. She had a good job; she was almost finished with law school; she wasn't desperate for male companionship. Yet she'd just gone above and beyond.

She probably appeared desperate.

She sighed and turned back toward the door. Yesterday Nora had brought over stew. Within a few days Tyler would have a refrigerator full of food, as various neighbors welcomed him with pies, cakes and other goodies. So what if she delivered her offering now? She'd use the opportunity to wiggle out of their date and nix this dumb idea she herself had come up with.

She opened the door and walked out. She'd just reached Tyler's driveway when, from out of nowhere, a black furry object launched itself at her, nose sniffing and mouth chomping for cookies.

"Tyler!" Kate yelled as long untrimmed nails

scratched at her clothes while the dog tried to maintain his two-legged stance while she backed up.

"Sport! Down!" Kate froze as the dog disobeyed the female voice.

"Sport! Down! Sit!" Tyler's voice boomed, and suddenly, the dog trotted away. "Ellen, get your dog into the backyard. Kate? Kate, are you okay?"

Someone removed the plate of cookies from her clenched fingers, and Tyler's arm settled on her shoulders. "Sorry about that. Let's get you home for a minute."

Kate let Tyler guide her back to her kitchen. "Don't tell me you have a dog," she said, trying to lower her heart rate.

"Nope. That's Leo and Ellen's monster. He's flunked every obedience class he's been in," Tyler added, kneeling next to the chair Kate had sat in so that they were at eye level. "He didn't hurt you too much, did he? I'm sorry about this. No one expects to walk out her kitchen door and get jumped."

"Maybe I should have looked twice the way Nora always insists." Kate slowed her breathing. "I'm not a dog person."

"Kate." Tyler's voice was soft as he gently pulled her hands away from her face. "I'm sorry. I didn't know you were afraid of dogs. If I had, I would have told Ellen to leave Sport at home."

"It's okay. We just don't have any dogs on Dogwood Lane. Sport caught me by surprise."

Tyler frowned, and Kate sensed he wasn't satisfied with her answer. His hands still covered hers and the warmth felt good, almost therapeutic. "Your hands are trembling."

"I'm not used to dogs," she repeated.

Without releasing her, Tyler settled himself at her feet. "It's more than that. Tell me."

Kate struggled for emotional and physical balance. How could he read her so well when he'd really just met her? She'd always kept her childhood secrets hidden, hadn't shared them with anyone except Sandra.

"You can trust me." Tyler's quiet voice washed over her. She hadn't felt strength like this since Sandra had been alive. Maybe she could confide in him. If nothing else, she'd learn his character immediately if he chose to run away.

"Once, when I was little, my mother told me to take the trash out and put it in the garage. My mom had some boyfriend over, one of the many nameless, faceless hordes of men revolving through her life. They were sitting at the kitchen table, beer cans all over."

Kate attempted to pull her hands from Tyler, but he only tightened his grasp.

"I opened the door to the garage like normal. All of a sudden some huge dog came running around the car, barking and snarling. When I dropped the trash bag, the dog bit me. I've been afraid ever since. It's probably irrational, because most dogs are friendly. I bet Sport is."

"Except around baked goods," Tyler said. "He's great with Leo's kids. With them he's calm and gentle."

"See?" Kate didn't protest as Tyler lowered her off the chair, down into his lap. She rested against him and he wove his fingers through her hair, stroking her scalp.

"What then?" Tyler asked.

"Sandra took me to the emergency room. The scars are hardly visible."

She held out her arm. Only faint streaks of white,

barely discernible, marred her skin. As he touched the scars with his forefinger, Tyler found himself angry. Normally, he was impassive, just recording the horrors he saw through his camera lens. But this was Kate. That someone had let her get hurt bothered him. Kate's physical scars might have faded, but her emotional scars would never heal.

"Sandra took care of you." Tyler's voice was husky.

"Yes," Kate managed to say. "Sandra called animal control. My mother was furious because her boyfriend blamed her for that. I'm not sure what else Sandra did, but I never lived with my mother again."

"She was indeed a special lady." Tyler stroked Kate's hair one last time before releasing her.

"She was." Kate fidgeted. Now that her shock had worn off, she was realizing the implications of this moment with Tylor. Not only had she been sitting in his lap, but she'd just told Tyler Nichols, a man she'd known less than two days, one of her worst life experiences. *And he hadn't run.*

Thing were getting way too deep too fast.

"Look, I'm fine." Kate stood and moved away to wash her hands in the sink. "Now that I've learned Sport is gentle, he won't surprise me again. You need to get back to your family. It's late."

Tyler noticed the wall clock and groaned. He stood. "It's past five! I've got to get them going, or we'll never get out of here."

"Tyler, we're not going out tonight."

"Of course we are." Tyler set his jaw in a stubborn line. "I'm not just saying that because you got a scare, either. I want to get to know you better, and not just because you're my neighbor."

Kate had never had her ego massaged this way, and it was amazing how good his attention felt. This gorgeous man—there was really no other better way to describe him—wanted to kick his family out of his house so he could take her out to eat.

After being in his arms, Kate had felt the strength and integrity at Tyler's core. Yet the moment was bittersweet. It always amazed her how people who grew up with wonderful families took them for granted, assumed they'd always be there. As Kate had discovered with Sandra, life didn't work that way. Sandra had gone much too soon. She'd never see Kate graduate law school or hold Kate's child. Kate bit her lip.

No, she resolved, she would not let Tyler take advantage of his family. He had one, even if he didn't fully appreciate how lucky he was. "Tyler." When she repeated his name, his brown eyes darkened. "We're not going out tonight. You're going home. You've been out of town, and you have to spend time with your family. They've missed you."

Tyler ran a hand up his nape. "I don't cancel dates."

"You aren't. I am."

He stared at her, and Kate wanted to swim in those warm chocolate eyes. Tyler Nichols—he was like a rock. But despite her need, she couldn't let him become her Gibraltar. She'd been alone for far too long to depend on anyone now. And Tyler's career was by nature too transient for him to have a permanent role in her life.

"Friends?" she said.

Tyler gave a short, resigned laugh that indicated he wasn't exactly pleased at the turn of events. "Yeah. Of course we are. I guess I should spend time with them."

"They drove all this way to help," Kate said. "Families are treasures. You're always out of town. You should enjoy their visit."

He seemed to realize she was comparing her situation with his. "You're right," he said with a sigh. "I'm being selfish. I just wanted to spend time with you."

"I understand and I'm flattered. So how big is your family?"

"Including me, four boys and one girl, my sisters-in-law, Ellen and Monica, and my nieces and nephews. Why don't you come and meet them? Well, all but the nieces and nephews and Monica. They're at her house."

Kate shook her head. "Thank you, but not today."

It was better not to meet his family, not to see what else she would never have. "I'll meet them some other time," she said softly, watching as disappointment etched Tyler's features.

His jaw tightened; his eyebrows drew closer, as if he was thinking. Finally, he nodded. "Okay. I'll look on the bright side, which is that this way I won't have to kill my brother Jamie for hitting on you. I don't want to get caught up in an assignment, so how about we go tomorrow?"

"Tomorrow?" Kate angled her head. So soon? Tyler certainly didn't let the grass grow under his feet.

"Tomorrow," Tyler confirmed. He walked to the door. "I'll be over. Same time?"

"Like I said, I have church in the morning with Frieda, and I didn't get very far on my Christmas lights. The neighbors always decorate to the nines."

"Okay," Tyler said, unconvinced. "Perhaps you could concentrate on this neighbor. Maybe accompany me to one of those home stores so I could get some lights? I'd hate to ruin the effect if every house is lit. Would it be better if we went earlier? Say, about two? A late lunch and shopping at the hardware store—that's not really a date at all."

Kate's chest tightened, part of her inwardly delighted that Tyler was continuing his pursuit of her. "A late lunch would be okay."

"I'll see you at two then." Tyler gave her a smile before he left.

Kate sat there a moment. She'd protected herself from being hurt for so long by hiding behind one shield or another. She'd do best to remember that Tyler wasn't going to be around long. Despite a definite interest on both their parts, he wasn't going to settle down and she wasn't going to settle for anything but.

She'd simply help him with his Christmas lights, allowing herself one date to remind herself she wasn't socially dead, so that when she told her friends she was dating someone, technically she wouldn't be lying. She exhaled slowly, absently petting Jeckyll after he jumped into her lap and started to purr.

As Tyler strode back inside his house, all seven people instantly fell silent. His mother, Leah, spoke first. "Is she all right, Tyler?"

"She's fine. She was a little shook up. That's all."

"Be sure to tell her I'm sorry," Ellen said. "You remember how Sport is about baked goods. Remember that whole strawberry cake he ate once? Ruined the entire birthday party. And I didn't know she was carrying cookies. He did pass obedience training on his last attempt."

"Barely," her husband, Leo, muttered.

Tyler tried to reassure his sister-in-law. "It's fine. Kate's already forgotten all about it."

"So is she coming back over?"

Tyler turned to Jamie. The last thing he needed was his lothario brother hitting on Kate. "No, she's not."

"So I guess we ruined your date, huh?" Craig gave Tyler a sympathetic look, one Tyler recognized as actually being in jest.

"It's okay. I know where she lives." Tyler shrugged.

"Yeah, I would guess you do," Jamie acknowledged. He stared at Tyler until Tyler broke the stare by turning away.

"I must have missed something. I thought all the people on this street were elderly," his sister, Tara, said. She'd arrived while Tyler had been at Kate's.

"Not all Tyler's neighbors are elderly," Craig said. "Tyler's next-door neighbor is in her late twenties. She's quite cute, and if you'd been here earlier, you could have seen both Tyler and Jamie fawning over her."

"I wasn't fawning," Jamie said with an easy, wolfish grin. "I was drooling. I wish I lived next to a good-looking neighbor who makes homemade cookies and lemonade. I'd be in heaven."

Jamie threw Tyler a daring glance, and Tyler bit his tongue. His mother was in the room, and she wouldn't approve of what he wanted to say.

"Well..." Craig spoke up. "I for one only came over to this dive because I was promised pizza. Speaking of which, if that pathetic excuse of a ringing noise I just heard was any indication, I'd say the food's here."

"Pizza?" Tyler asked.

"Yeah, I took the liberty of ordering while you were

next door," Craig said. "Where's your wallet? We installed all these things, so you're buying."

Four hours later Tyler's living room was finally empty of his family. The evening had been a typical one. Once again he'd seen the hopeful expression on his mother's face when he told her he'd be in town for a bit, and then he'd seen it fade when he'd reminded her he never stayed long.

His mother would never understand his wanderlust. Tyler wanted to be Photographer of the Year; heck, he'd even settle for a Pulitzer. The stuff he'd shot in Iraq was definitely worthy.

So, once again the night had ended with his mother reminding Tyler of the dangers. "I still don't like it," Leah had said. "I read about some journalists who got shot, one even maimed. And remember that man in Bosnia who got in his car and it exploded when he turned the key? He lost his legs—"

"Leah." His father had cut off the conversation, and at that point Tyler had kissed his mother goodbye.

Tyler peeled the label off his bottle of beer. The brew was long warm; he'd just dump the remaining half out. Without the presence of his tight-knit family, his small house seemed big and empty. Tyler began throwing away the remains of dinner. He wiped down the entire counter using those premoistened kitchen wipes his mother had brought over. Then he allowed himself to look across the driveway. Except for the Christmas twinkling lights on her porch, Kate's bungalow was quiet. If she was home, she was on the other side of the house, because her kitchen window was dark.

He mulled over what Kate had told him about her childhood. As a photojournalist, he knew life wasn't fair. He hoped his photos would make the world sit up and take notice of man's atrocities, but beyond that he really had no control.

Darn. He threw the wipe in the trash can. Nothing and no one ever wormed their way under his skin, yet in about twenty-four hours Kate had burrowed deep. He glanced at her darkened windows again and brought his chin up with new determination. As Scarlett had said, tomorrow was another day.

FROM ACROSS THE STREET, Nora watched as the lights in Tyler's house flickered off one by one. He was finally going to bed. Most of the other Dogwood Lane residents had already settled in for the night, their Christmas lights keeping the street aglow. She'd have to tell Tyler to get some lights and resolved to do that tomorrow after church. His house was the only one without some sort of lawn ornamentation or light decorations.

Satisfied nothing else was amiss, Nora let her aluminum blinds snap shut. She reached for the cup of tea she'd set near the window and took a sip. She simply didn't trust Tyler Nichols. He'd had quite a crowd of people over tonight, obviously forgetting all about his date with Kate. Her lights had gone out hours ago. She'd worked in her yard most of the day. When Nora had popped over, Kate had said she'd finish the lights tomorrow. At that time, she'd still been going to dinner.

It hadn't happened. Neither her car nor Tyler's had left the driveway. In fact, Nora had observed a pizza deliveryman drive up.

Nora took another sip, trying to let the chamomile soothe her. However, she remained agitated. All Frieda had talked about during their gin game this afternoon was Tyler. That Frieda. She'd become a menace lately, especially where Kate was concerned. Everyone else on Dogwood Lane understood that Niles—not this new fellow across the way who forgot his promises and skipped out on dinner—was perfect for Kate. As she removed the binoculars off her neck, placed them on the windowsill and went to bed, she contemplated what to do about it.

THE NEXT MORNING Kate scrutinized herself in the mirror as she ran a brush through her hair one final time before she left to get Frieda.

Today was her date with Tyler. At that thought, Kate sobered and frowned at her reflection. In the morning, doubt had crept back in. She was nothing special. So why exactly did Tyler Nichols want to spend time with her? Compared with him, she was an absolute nobody.

Since she'd canceled dinner, she'd had time to go into her home office last night and work on her research paper. When she was mostly finished, curiosity had bested her and she'd used her computer to locate as much information as she could on Tyler. She'd Googled him and searched her law school's online databases.

The results had been mostly photo credits—his work had accompanied at least twenty stories that she'd found on various news-media Web sites. What she'd seen had been impressive, visionary.

As Kate stepped out of the bathroom, Jeckyll wove himself in between her legs, a sure sign his food dish was empty. In the kitchen, Kate glanced at the microwave clock. She had a few minutes before picking Frieda up and taking her to church.

The phone shrilled, shattering the silence. Kate checked the caller ID and answered. "Hi, Nora."

"Just checking to make sure you're remembering Frieda. Until she gets her new glasses, she shouldn't be driving anywhere."

"I haven't forgotten. I'm about to get her now."

"Good," Nora said. "Oh, while I've got you on the phone, you're attending Christmas Eve service with me, right?"

"It's already on my calendar," Kate said, balancing the cordless phone against her ear as she grabbed a single-serving container of cottage cheese from the refrigerator. She'd been trying to eat healthier, especially after indulging at Frieda's Thanksgiving feast. Ever since Kate had moved in with Sandra, the three matrons had alternated various holiday events, from the Fourth of July to Halloween. After Sandra's death, Kate had continued the tradition. There was comfort in rituals, and this year Easter was at her house, provided Nora and Frieda were in town and available for dinner.

"So what happened to your plans?" Nora asked.

"I canceled. His family came over and helped install new appliances."

"Oh. I wondered who those people were."

Kate spooned cottage cheese into her mouth and waited. Nora wasn't through.

"Probably for the best. He's trouble, if you ask me. He'll need to put up Christmas lights, but he'll never be here to turn them on. How's that going to work?"

Kate swallowed. "I'll ask him when we go shopping for decorations today."

Kate could almost envision Nora rolling her eyes.

"Don't get involved with him, Kate. No one wants to see you hurt again," Nora said.

"I'll be fine. I've got to go pick up Frieda or we'll be late. I'll talk to you later." Kate disconnected, and tossed the empty cottage-cheese container in the trash.

She managed to put Tyler out of her mind until the ride home, when Frieda asked, "So where do you think he'll take you?"

"I don't know," Kate said. Because she'd attended a 9:00 a.m. service, the morning was still young. "It's just a lunch and shopping at Lowe's or Home Depot. Nothing that exciting. I have some final Christmas decorations to put up first and it's going to be a gorgeous day."

"This weather is crazy," Frieda said, latching on to the new topic. "It's December second, and we're getting eighty-degree temperatures while Denver's getting another two feet of snow. At least it's not happening at peak holiday travel time, like last year."

"That was awful," Kate agreed. Not only had highways shut down, but the Denver airport had been closed for days. Luckily, Frieda had arrived at her son's the previous day.

"Maybe we do have global warming," Frieda said. "Did you see Al Gore's movie, *An Inconvenient Truth?*"

"I have to admit I haven't had time," Kate said.

"It's been out more than a year," Frieda chided. She paused a moment as she remembered. "Oh, that's right, you never see many movies. I have them delivered to my door. Anyway, thanks for taking me today. Darned insurance for seniors means I can't get my glasses until tomorrow. Had to wait until the month changed. Now I'll have to wait for them to get made."

"It's no problem," Kate said as they reached Dogwood Lane. "I enjoyed the service. Quite different from what I normally attend when I go with Nora." Kate had pretty much stopped going to church once Sandra had passed away, but occasionally she worked it in.

"Yes, we're rather contemporary in our choice of music and worship style," Frieda said. "Now, you have a great time with Tyler today. Don't let him get away from you."

"It's just lunch. Nothing special," Kate reiterated.

"You have to eat," Frieda insisted. "Might as well do it with a hot man."

"Frieda, it's not like I need a date to dine out," Kate protested. "I have other things in my life to worry about than free food."

"Honey, you have to keep your foot in the door," Frieda said. "Did I ever tell you how I met my Charles? I wasn't looking for anyone. I'd just started my first job as a secretary and one of my duties was to accept the mail. Charlie was a postal carrier. It took him only three weeks before he asked me out. Six months afterward we were engaged, and a year later married. I quit work when I got pregnant."

"I want to work," Kate said. "I'm not interested in getting married. I haven't even had my career yet. I've been forking out tons of money for this law degree. I don't plan to have a diploma that simply hangs on the wall. I want to pass the bar and start practicing."

"Which is all fine and good," Frieda said. Kate had pulled in to Frieda's driveway and the elderly lady opened the passenger door the moment Kate put the gear into Park. "No one is saying you can't have it all. In fact, your generation has opportunities available to you that mine never had. Grasp all of them. But you do have to admit, Tyler is some sweet eye candy. Like I said, if I were forty years younger…"

"I will admit that he's good-looking," Kate agreed.

"Honey, he's a god."

Kate laughed, waved goodbye to Frieda and drove the short distance home. Within minutes she'd changed clothes and begun her outside work. She flicked a glance over at Tyler's house. He was there if the Hummer sitting in the driveway was an indication.

Yesterday she'd gotten most of her holiday decorations up, but because she'd gardened and baked cookies, she hadn't finished. She opened the box of lights she'd bought. She'd have some left over that she could give him.

In the spirit of being neighborly, of course.

Who was she kidding? She was being more than neighborly. Lemonade. Cookies. Lights. Lunch. Way too deep already. She had to be careful. Already he'd upended her world. Being with him was like playing with fire. Searing. Dangerous. Destructive. Tempting. Yet it was futile to think she'd ever get what she wanted.

She should just tell Wendy the truth on Monday. Call off the whole charade, including the date today.

"Hi," he said.

Too late.

Chapter Six

Hours later, a little after three-thirty, Kate stepped from Tyler's Hummer and gazed up at the brick building housing the Orlando Bottleworks and Pub.

"Ready?" Tyler came around and closed her door.

"Yes." She followed him into the stand-alone brick building. They still had the home-decorating store left to go to, but the back of his SUV was already loaded with purchases from the home-improvement warehouse. Her stomach growled. Because she'd snacked after church, they'd chosen to shop first, eat second, then shop more.

"Thanks for agreeing to this place," Tyler said as they entered the microbrewery. "This is one of my favorite places and I haven't been here in ages. It's a real treat."

As they walked past the metal brewing tanks and approached the hostess desk, the industrial-chic ambience was evident. Soon she and Tyler were seated across from each other in a booth toward the back of the room.

"I can understand why you like it here," Kate said. She sank into the comfortable green vinyl cushion of their booth, which butted the exposed-brick wall. Christmas lights wrapped in garland twinkled from the balcony surrounding the open, multistory area they were seated in. The restaurant had been decked out. "This place is pretty cool."

"Glad you like it," Tyler said.

"You know, I never would have chosen somewhere like this," Kate admitted.

"The microbrewery is pretty nondescript on the outside," Tyler agreed.

"But inside is atmosphere galore. Look at those wood beams. If the food lives up to the decor, you've done well." She picked up her menu.

Tyler used a forefinger and pushed her menu down. His eyes, visible over the menu, had depth, soul. "It'll live up to it. I'm a man of my word."

"I'll keep that in mind," she said, defusing his seriousness. She'd had such fun already today she didn't want to blow the moment now. They'd gotten her lights finished in half the time, and they'd laughed and mock-argued as they'd searched the hardware store. He hadn't spared any expense, even buying a ladder so he could reach the roof.

She put the menu back up in front of her face and tried to concentrate when Tyler's leg accidentally connected with hers under the table.

Tyler suddenly leaned over the menu she was staring blankly at. "If you're still planning on having a beer to spite Nora, then I'll recommend this lager right here."

"The gold?" Kate asked. She blinked, for Tyler's face, despite the width of the wooden table, was in proximity to hers, his lips even nearer.

"Right. The gold." He pointed to another item on her menu. "For something lighter, though not too light, you can try this, the pale. I've had it, and it's very good."

When Tyler settled himself back down on his seat,

Kate contemplated the menu again. She finally ordered the pale lager when the waitress wrote down their drink order. Tyler settled for the black, a beer akin to the color of melted tar.

"Well?" Tyler gazed expectantly over the rim of his glass. His lips rested on the edge, and Kate shifted in her seat as she sipped the beer she'd chosen.

"It's good." It was, and Kate wiped the foam off the top of her lip. Normally, she wouldn't have had any alcohol before supper, but it was close enough. Besides, as the song said, it was five o'clock somewhere.

"I'm glad you like it," Tyler remarked. He tapped his fingers on the table before taking another taste of his own.

"It's excellent, in fact," Kate said, suddenly experiencing a sense of déjà vu. She hadn't been on a "date" in more than a year. That evening hadn't been a great time, with many awkward silences falling.

So what did one talk about on a date? Now that she and Tyler were almost free of chores like decorating and picking out lights, would she turn back into a pumpkin? Most of the men on her previous dates had found her uninteresting. Few wanted to talk politics or legal issues—the things she knew a great deal about. She didn't care much for television shows and had never seen an episode of the current popular sitcom.

Tyler stepped up to the plate. "Just a few suggestions. Anything they wood-fire is fantastic, especially the pizza. Although I'm not having it today, I have had it before, and it's great."

"I was thinking about the five-cheese personal pizza," Kate said. It sounded delicious.

"You won't regret it," Tyler said, settling for a steak himself.

"So," Tyler began slowly as the waitress whisked their menus away.

"So," Kate parroted, reaching for her beer and taking a drink as an excuse for not having anything else to say.

Tyler didn't seem to mind and easily picked up the slack. "Thanks for helping me get my lights. I'll put them up tomorrow."

"You're not working?"

He shook his head. "My job isn't nine to five. I might be on an assignment seven days a week, twenty-four hours a day for a few months. Like this past job. As I told you, I followed a marine unit around."

"And they just accept you?"

"Yes and no," Tyler said. "You become friendly with someone, but since I'm not a marine, I'm an outsider. I become like a fly on the wall. They know I'm there, but they ignore me. Not that we don't talk or anything. But no bonds form."

"I guess like a reality show," Kate said. She had seen an episode or two of *Survivor,* but she didn't follow the show religiously. "They have cameras filming everything, but there's to be no interaction between the contestants and the crew."

"Yes, I guess that's sort of how my job is," he said. "I'm there living with them, but I'm not part of their social circle. They don't include me in their card games, for instance."

"Must be lonely."

"I've never thought about it like that," Tyler said, his forehead creasing as he contemplated her statement. "Not all jobs have dividing lines. When I climbed Everest, I was a member of an expedition. My job was to document the climb, but I was in charge of a bunch of other things, as well. Everyone had to pull equal weight."

"Everest," Kate said. He'd risked his life climbing a snow-covered mountain in the Himalayas.

"You think I'm crazy," Tyler said.

"I'm going to reserve judgment," she said with a shake of her head. "But I bet you've been told that before."

"Constantly. Sometimes people are impressed, but sometimes they give me the look you're sending my way now."

Kate shook her head. "I'm not the adventurous type," she said. "I don't even ride the roller coasters at theme parks."

"What? They're the best part," Tyler said. "I hit them all. The faster and steeper, the better."

"Not me. I'd much rather be on the carousel. I guess I'm not a risk taker," Kate said. The waitress arrived with her salad and Kate poured the dressing, which had been served on the side in a small cup. "I mean, you're doing Russian dressing and I've got basic boring ranch."

"Nothing wrong with ranch. It's my second favorite," Tyler said.

"So I guess your job takes you everywhere."

"Yes, I admit to having filled quite a few passports. I've been everywhere except Antarctica. I won't bore you with the details. In the end, it's just a job and a lot of hotel rooms. I hope to make a difference by providing the visuals. That's my objective, anyway."

"It's a good goal to have," Kate said, relieved that they had at least this much in common. "That's why I want to be a family-law lawyer. Maybe I can keep some-one from going through what I did."

"That's noble," Tyler said.

Kate studied him for second to be sure he was seri-ous. He was. "Thanks," she said. "Lawyers don't have very good reputations. Most people think I decided to be in the legal profession so I can make a lot of money. San-dra left me a small inheritance. While it's not enough to afford a life of leisure, it's enough that I won't have to suffer working at a job I hate."

"I'm a firm believer that your career has to be some-thing you love. That's why I do what I do," Tyler said.

"I saw some of your work on the Internet," Kate admitted after their entrées had been served. "You're good."

"Thanks." Tyler cut into his steak and popped a bite into his mouth. "Oh, I've missed this. The Europeans just don't grill steaks the way we do."

"I thought you were in Iraq."

"I was. But I had a layover in Germany. As much as possible, I try to eat local food when I'm traveling. I'm not one of those tourists who has to find a McDonald's."

"I've never even left Florida," Kate said.

He seemed surprised. "No?"

She shook her head. "The beach is as far as I've got-ten, and that was only once. I'm not very worldly."

"That's nothing to be ashamed of," he said. "Most Americans generally don't travel as much as the Euro-peans do. We don't have the vacation time they do. We also put our money into our larger houses, tying up a lot of it."

"You're too kind," Kate said. "It bothers me, though. When I'm out of school and working, I'm definitely going to travel. First stop, Washington, D.C. The White House. The Lincoln Memorial. The entire Smithsonian."

"Be sure to take lots of pictures," Tyler teased.

"Yeah, right. I wish. I'm not even able to get decent pictures with my camera. Besides, all I do is point and shoot."

"Digital set on automatic?" Tyler asked.

"Yes," Kate said. "I thought about taking a basic photography class at the community college, but with law school I haven't had the time. Maybe next year."

They'd finished eating and Tyler handed his credit card to the waitress.

"You know, I could teach you a few things to make your pictures come out better," Tyler said. "Even if you leave your camera set on automatic, you can still get great shots. A lot of it is in how you compose the picture."

"Like I said, I just aim and click."

"That's half your problem. One of the most basic rules of composition is this simple. You don't place anything dead center. Instead, you put the most important thing in your shot slightly off center."

"Interesting," she said. "I learn something new every day."

Tyler signed his charge slip and pocketed his credit card. "Shall we?"

Kate slid from the booth. "Thanks for lunch. I told you I'd pay my half."

"And I got it. You can buy next time."

"Okay." She nodded, oddly comfortable being with him. Tyler didn't make her nervous or make her feel she wasn't good enough. She felt respected, listened to. "Okay," she agreed. "The next outing is on me."

HE'D NEVER MET anyone quite like Kate. Here he was, in the middle of the Christmas decorations at one of those oversize home-decorating centers. The Christmas-tree displays, with their millions of twinkling lights, simply didn't hold a candle to her. She—as cheesy at it sounded—glowed. Her smile was infectious. He doubted any other woman would want to be here with him, purchasing cartfuls of Christmas goods. He'd needed everything. He didn't even have a fake tree.

They rounded a corner. "Oh," she said.

In the center of the aisle was a huge, six-foot-tall, inflatable snow globe. Inside was a movable North Pole diorama. She approached and studied it. "Wow."

"Amazing what they can make these days," Tyler replied. "Like it?"

"I do."

"You should get it."

Kate fingered the tag, read the price and shook her head. "Too much. Maybe next year. As long as I've got my lights up I'm fine."

Tyler glanced at the price tag. "I could get it and put it in my yard."

"You're already putting everything else on a timer," Kate said. "Lights are fine if you're not going to be around."

As they walked down the next aisle, her comment ate at him. True, he wouldn't be around. But he liked the inflatable snow globe. She liked it. "What if I get it and you keep it in your yard when I'm gone?"

She shook her head. They'd reached the artificial Christmas trees. "That's okay. Really, I'm good. But I will get a few more ornament hangers while I'm here. I don't remember—do you have a tree?"

He arched an eyebrow and she laughed, answering her own question. "No, I didn't think you did."

"I do like Christmas," Tyler protested. "I'm just never around." Even to his ears that sounded like a lame excuse. Missing the holiday had never bothered him. Attempting to divert Kate's attention from his shortcomings, he said, "Now, my mom—she does the whole shebang. The entire house looks like a spread in one of those women's magazines. Not one inch is left untouched. If I photographed that type of stuff, I wouldn't have to travel far at all."

"Sandra used to decorate every inch. I have a lot of her stuff, but it's simply so time-consuming to get it all out. I do set up the tree and all the ornaments."

"My mom got us kids a new ornament every year," Tyler said.

"Sandra did, too!" Kate added a box of ornament hangers to the cart. "She'd wrap it and tell me Santa brought it. Even after I stopped believing. That was her thing."

"These days my mom buys them for the grandchildren," Tyler said. "She divided up each of our ornaments and gave us half of them so we could decorate our own trees. My box is still at her house."

"Then get a tree," Kate said. She pointed to one of the prelit, artificial ones. "These are easy to put up and take down."

"Okay. I'll do it, but on one condition. I've heard decorating requires a woman's touch. Will you help me?"

"Um…" Kate stood there, not sure how to answer. Decorating seemed like crossing an invisible line.

He sensed her uncertainty. "It'll be easy. Go pick out some tinsel or beads or whatever you stick on a tree.

I'm seeing boxes of ornaments over there. Don't I need a theme or something?"

She shot him an "are you crazy" glance. "I go for the haphazard look."

Tyler remembered one woman he'd dated. Her tree had had everything perfectly positioned, as if she'd used a ruler to measure out the distance between the rows of tinsel. "Random sounds perfect."

A salesperson walked by at that moment and stopped and asked if he could help. "I'm going to take one of these trees." Tyler said. "I'm also going to need another cart."

"Let me get a flatbed," the teenage boy said, darting off.

Kate nodded her approval. "Your first real Christmas. Go pick out some ornaments you might like. I'll get some tinsel."

She headed off to the end of the aisle. As if sensing he was watching her, she glanced back at him, a quizzical expression on her face. He quickly turned away, his attention on the huge array of ornaments in front of him.

There were far too many choices. He had no idea what to get. He liked the shiny red glass balls like the ones his mother had, so he placed two boxes of those in the cart. There were some white snowflakes, so he added them. He moved down the aisle, occasionally placing something in his cart. When he reached the end, he found a display of individual ornaments akin to those found at a card shop.

At eye height was a tiny snow globe. Inside was a miniature Christmas tree with presents under it. He peeked down the aisle. Kate had grabbed a spare cart and was loading things into it. He picked up the snow globe. She'd love this.

The boy came back with the flatbed, the Christmas tree already loaded up. "I want this, too," Tyler said, holding out his hand. "Take everything up to the front. I don't want her to see the ornament."

"Gotcha." The boy quickly walked away.

Within minutes Kate was next to Tyler, her cart filled with tinsel. "I think we're good," she said.

"Awesome," Tyler said. "Let's pay for this stuff."

They had almost reached the checkout when he stopped. "Wait. I forgot batteries."

"I'll get them," Kate said.

Tyler slid the ornament through first, then hid the bag under his coat before Kate returned.

A little less than an hour later, he and Kate were decorating his tree. She'd been ready to go to her place once they'd arrived back on Dogwood Lane. Not ready for the date to end yet, he'd convinced her to stay.

"You're staring at me," Kate said, her fingers poised to place the last strand of tinsel on the tree.

"Have you ever thought of modeling?" he asked. Her grace was as natural to her as breathing.

"Oh, please," Kate scoffed. "That's for those pretty, six-foot-tall women who blow away in a light wind."

"Not necessarily," Tyler said. "It's all about camera angles. Here. I'll show you." He left the room and returned a moment later with his camera bag. As he opened it, Kate came over.

"That's a lot of lenses," she observed.

"Yep," Tyler said, taking out the camera and selecting a lens. "Each one does something different." He pointed to a long one. "That's for zooming in more than fifty feet. That one there gives me a wider angle." He connected a shorter lens. "This one will be perfect. Now, go back to what you were doing."

Kate shook her head. "Really, I—"

"No, let me show you what I mean. Just go hang some ornaments. The blue ones. They'll match your eyes." Kate appeared hesitant. "The camera's digital. We'll delete everything. Promise."

That convinced her to play along. She went over and began to hang ornaments. "Just act normal," he told her, adjusting the camera to the light. "You'll hear clicking. Ignore it."

He lowered his eye to the viewfinder. He'd been right. She was beyond pretty. He snapped off ten shots and then moved into a different position. She'd never believe him if he didn't show her what else a camera could do. He snapped two more pictures. "Okay, come see."

Kate put the ornament she'd just picked up back into the box and sat next to him on the couch. Tyler fiddled with some buttons. "I'll show you the ugly shots first."

"Great," Kate said, leaning over for a better view.

"A photographer has the power to alter reality," Tyler said, displaying the first image.

"You made my butt look big!" Kate exclaimed. "Delete that. Right now."

Tyler laughed and did what he was told. "You don't want a big old booty?"

"No woman wants a big old booty," Kate said, edging closer for a better view of the next shot. "Hmm."

"This one's nothing special," Tyler said. Her leg had moved next to his and he liked it. "This one doesn't do you justice. It's just an average snapshot, like the ones most people take." He pressed a button, deleting it. "Now, these…" He angled the camera so she could view the next image. "This is how I see you."

SHE LOOKED BEAUTIFUL. Whatever magic the camera wrought, Tyler had captured a side of herself she'd never seen.

She still wore the same white long-sleeved T-shirt covered by a holiday sweater. Her hair hadn't changed color and she hadn't put on any fancy makeup, just her normal everyday cosmetics.

"Like them?" he asked, showing her the other pictures he'd taken. They, too, caught her at her best. "Want me to delete these or burn them to a CD for you?"

"I…" Her survival instinct screamed at her to run for cover, but her rationality won. "That would be great, thank you."

"Thank *you*," Tyler said. He set the camera down on the coffee table and faced her. "I've had a great day. I've really enjoyed this."

"We haven't even finished your tree," Kate protested as he inched closer. His body against hers sent all sorts of delightful signals.

"I'm going to kiss you now," he told her, and although she opened her mouth to protest, not one word came out as his lips came down.

She'd never been kissed like this. Why was it that the man you couldn't have permanently kissed the best? Like his photographs of her, Tyler's lips gave her a different perspective on life. She lost herself in him—until her cell phone rang.

"Leave it," he urged.

She pulled away, the intrusion welcome. Kissing Tyler was like ingesting a mind-altering drug. She was fast losing control of common sense. She'd known the man only a few days, yet it was as if she'd wanted him all her life, and if he kept kissing her, she'd allow him to lead her anywhere. "It's Frieda's ring tone. I've got to take the call."

She stood, but by the time she'd reached her purse, her phone beeped, indicating she had a message. "I should probably go," Kate said. "I've enjoyed this."

He tilted his head; the man was pure charm. "You won't stay and help me finish?"

"Best if I leave," Kate replied, easing toward the kitchen. "I still have a lot of studying to do tonight. Finals are soon."

He nodded. "I understand. We'll have to do this again sometime. I mean, go out."

"Uh, yeah. If you're in town. I understand that you'll be gone a lot," Kate said. She'd entered the kitchen and she grabbed her coat. "I'll see you around, and thanks for helping me out. Now I guess I can say we've had a date."

"Yeah," Tyler said. He stood there, arms crossed, and Kate shifted her weight, eager to leave.

"So you're still planning on telling everyone you're dating me?" he asked.

"I'm positive Wendy will have told everyone why I missed the party. I'm not planning on telling anyone directly, but I'm not correcting anyone. It'll all blow over really quickly. You know how office gossip is," she hedged, hand on the doorknob.

He nodded and Kate got the impression he hadn't liked her answer. She gave him a small smile. "I really appreciate you doing this. This will buy me time to get this semester under my belt. And it's not as though you really want to date me. You won't be around, and neither of us has time. Plus, we live right next door. That could get awkward. You don't mind just being friends, do you?"

He didn't respond, and she opened the door, afraid she'd suddenly grown three heads. "I'm sure I'll see you tomorrow or something."

With that, she quickly shut the door behind her and escaped.

Chapter Seven

"So how was your date?" Frieda asked when she called back less than ten minutes later. Kate had barely gotten inside when her home phone had started shrilling.

"It was fine," she answered. "We went shopping and to lunch. That's it. Nothing more."

"He didn't kiss you?" Frieda questioned, her disappointment clear through the connection.

"No," Kate lied, "so if Nora's there with you, tell her nothing happened. There's nothing to gossip about."

"Darn. I thought there'd be at least some juicy details. Nora will be here in a few minutes. We're going over to Harold's for bunco. You want to join us?"

"Thanks, but no," Kate said. "I've got a final tomorrow night and need to review. I also have to finish my paper. You two have fun."

"We will," Frieda said.

Kate hung up the phone and smiled. Frieda and Nora were like Oscar and Felix. Opposites, but so in sync with each other. Best friends, worst enemies, they'd seen each other through everything, including their beloved spouses' respective deaths.

Maybe opposites really did attract. Today she'd been nervous, yet she'd had such a great time with Tyler. He'd climbed Everest, and she'd never set foot outside of Florida. They clicked as if they'd known each other all their lives. He'd kissed her. Made her look beautiful. Maybe that was what life and love were all about. Finding that person who accepted you for exactly who you were.

Except Tyler Nichols wasn't going to be around long. That was why she'd been so nervous when saying goodnight and goodbye. Friends. That would be best. Safest. She wasn't in this to find herself a man but to get the matchmakers off her back. Besides, Tyler didn't fit her criteria. She wanted nine to five. Weekends off to do things. Not gone three months at a stretch in Iraq.

She glanced at his house and rang Frieda back. "Tell Nora that Tyler will put his lights up tomorrow. He bought tons of stuff, including a ladder. She can go inspect his handiwork while I'm at the office."

Frieda laughed. "I'll tell her."

Kate hung up, grabbed a bottle of water and banished Tyler from her thoughts. She had a paper to proofread.

TYLER TAPPED on the remote control. Normally, he enjoyed watching *60 Minutes,* but tonight he couldn't focus.

Instead, his gaze kept straying out the sliding patio door of his den. Darkness had descended on Orlando, and across the way, light from Kate's bedroom windows filtered out onto her lawn. At least, he assumed it was light from her bedroom.

Then again, maybe she'd converted the back bedroom into an office the way he had. Whatever the room's use, the light indicated her presence. And it was driving him crazy.

He wanted her.

He'd kissed her. Perhaps it had been best that she'd gotten that phone call, because once he'd started kissing Kate, he hadn't wanted to stop.

Although, she had shut him down cold. In the kitchen she'd done a complete one-eighty. She'd put on her coat and been ready to head out the door. He'd been pathetic. Resisting another urge to pull her back into his arms and kiss her, he'd lamely asked that question about whether she planned on telling people about their date. He should have been better prepared for her reaction. Instead, he'd been hoping she'd reconsider. But Kate hadn't said anything to contradict him.

He hadn't liked the "just friends" label one bit. He'd gone shopping with her—and he hated shopping. Sure, one store had been a testosterone-filled home-improvement warehouse, but still. He'd shopped with a female other than his mother or sister—and he'd enjoyed it. He'd tucked her ornament away for Christmas.

That was why her "you don't mind" irked him. It shouldn't have, but it did. After all, he was the wanderer. He wasn't a homebody looking to settle down. So why had he bought her anything at all?

He headed back into the living room. His tree stood partially decorated, and he simply didn't have the desire to finish it. He picked up his camera and turned it on, an image of Kate flickering to life on the rectangular screen.

Damn it, what was he doing? He was supposed to be just the guy who helped her out of a matchmaking jam. Yet he'd found himself powerless not to kiss her. She called to something primal inside him. He knew how wrong he was for her, but being with Kate was like photographing a freight-train wreck. He simply couldn't turn away.

What did he have to offer Miss Home and Hearth besides some fantastic chemistry? Sure, he had money, all of it invested and earning compound interest and dividends. But Kate didn't care about money. She valued those intangible things like stability and love. She was the type who wanted forever, the type who deserved a man who would wake up beside her every morning.

Tyler couldn't be that. He traveled. He'd never been a forty-hour-a-week guy in his life. If he hadn't been forced to buy property to keep the IRS from bleeding him dry, he would never have stepped foot onto Dogwood Lane.

He left behind the slivers of light shining on her backyard and strode into the kitchen to grab a beer out of his new, yet mostly empty, refrigerator. At some point he'd have to buy basics like ketchup and mustard. His refrigerator was normally pretty bare. Usually, when not on assignment, he ate out.

He took a long swallow and stared out the window. Kate's kitchen window was dark, meaning she was probably studying, her nose in whatever text was required for passing her upcoming law test. Oblivious to his frustration, she'd probably cracked open her law books without giving him a second thought.

Tyler took another long swallow and let the chilled liquid slide down his throat. Instead of making him feel better, the cold beer caused a tiny headache to form between his eyes.

He had to be realistic. She didn't want him. But he wanted her, and not just because she was a challenge. Tyler frowned and took another sip, headache be damned.

However, he didn't want to be her mythical man, the one fabricated to keep the matchmakers at bay. No, he wanted to guide her into his bed and explore the chemistry between them. He wanted to make love to her for hours, until both of them were so exhausted they slept for days. He always followed his instincts, and this time his gut told him that whatever feelings he had for Kate Merrill, they were unlike any he'd ever had.

Tyler drained the beer and shook the empty bottle. Briefly, he contemplated having another one, but with a shrug he tossed the bottle into the trash can. He wasn't one to drink away his dilemmas. He'd seen enough people do just that, only to learn the hard way that problems could swim.

The ringing of his cell phone came as a blessed intervention, and as he looked at the caller identification, he gave a grin of relief.

"Tyler Nichols."

"Ty!" The bubbly voice on the end of the line was as familiar to Tyler as his mother's. "I got you."

"Hey, Jess. Been wondering when you'd break down and call me. Whatcha baiting me with this time?"

"How about a paid trip to California? And if you're really good, I'll let you stop by Hollywood on the way home and pick up a wannabe starlet."

"You know how good I am." Tyler cradled the phone to his ear. Having worked together for more than ten years, he and his assignment editor had developed their own communication style. "Tell me more."

"David Gregory's doing an enterprise piece on how California has changed since Arnold won the governorship. He's going to look back at the five years Arnold's been in office and focus on what's upcoming in the next three."

"Length of stay?"

"How about a week or two? Maximum. That should do it. Home by Christmas."

Tyler glanced at Kate's house. "I promised my mother this year that I'd be present for the annual Nichols holiday dinner. Make sure I am, okay?"

"Will do."

"When do I leave?"

"I'm working on flights now. There's no urgency, so you're flying commercial instead of charter. I'll call you back when I have all the details."

"Get me out of here later in the day. I've got to put my Christmas lights up tomorrow morning."

"Christmas lights?"

"You heard I bought a house, didn't you? The whole neighborhood has them. Not one spot on the block without. Since I'll be gone, I'm going to have to put mine on a timer. I guess I'll get one of those in the morning."

"You'd be the sore thumb if you didn't," Jess pointed out.

"Yeah, and I just moved in," Tyler replied. "Not a very good impression on the neighbors. My only saving grace is that the lady living here before me went into a retirement home and all the grandmothers on the block see me as a prime matchmaking target."

"I'll schedule you a late-afternoon flight," Jess said. "Well, I don't need you in trouble with the senior set. Wow. You being domestic. That's pretty scary. You do know that, don't you?"

"'Night, Jess." Tyler pushed the end button on his

cell phone and smiled. The nice thing about his job was that he could live anywhere so long as he could board an airplane. Tyler stretched and immediately the melancholy lifted. Tomorrow he'd be on his way west. His blood flowed in anticipation. Then he gazed over at Kate's window.

Probably for the best that he hadn't continued to kiss her. Work was his mistress, and she'd just come knocking.

After an hour of studying, Kate pushed the divorce-case-study book away and rubbed both temples with her forefingers. She hated reviewing divorce-case history, but it was a necessary evil for her future as a family lawyer. She'd like to specialize in adoptions. Still, she'd probably handle a few divorces, as well. While she wished every marriage would end in happily-ever-after, fifty percent wouldn't. That was why she'd been so determined not to rush into a relationship herself. Like with Tyler. Even though she'd connected with him, how could they make anything work?

Jeckyll shifted in the middle of the chair and opened one eye to regard Kate at her desk. When he meowed, Kate groaned. She just didn't want to read any more law. Worse, ever since her date, she hadn't been able to concentrate. Tyler rattled her.

Kate placed her elbows on the desk and her head in her hands. She'd dubbed Tyler her "fake date" for work purposes only. One kiss had proven he was anything but.

He was definitely flesh and blood. Just thinking about him caused tingles to spread through her. Darn

Wendy for planting that "go have passionate sex" idea. Tyler was a temptation Kate didn't need.

Kate stood and stretched. Being with Tyler made her feel alive. Being with Jack had been like being with three-day-old soda pop—flat and lifeless. With Tyler her blood actually zinged. Kissing him was like eating a piece of gourmet chocolate cake. Delicious, decadent and never large enough for true satisfaction. She wanted more.

Best that no more kisses occurred.

Not even to forever erase Jack's memory in all areas could she succumb to the passion of Tyler. She determined to push aside any thoughts of making love to him.

Kate left her office and made her way to the kitchen, where she flipped on the light, chasing away the shadows that had long ago crept into the room. Jeckyll wandered in behind her and, upon seeing that Kate wasn't refilling his food bowl, found a corner near a heat register and went back to sleep.

A light knock sounded at the door. Tyler? Her heart fluttering, she flung open the door.

"How many times do I have to tell you not to do that?" Kate moved back to let Nora enter. "I figured I'd stop by after bunco and check on you."

"Hello, Nora." Kate kept her voice steady.

"Hello, dear." Nora seemed to float in, her shawl flowing behind her. "Frieda said you helped Tyler at the hardware store. So that's where you went. I saw you get into his car. Didn't you have schoolwork to do?"

"I'm studying now. Just taking a break. I can only sit in a chair for so long."

"Oh." Nora frowned, the silver chain on her glasses shaking. "So it was a nice date?"

Kate sighed. Nora was like two or three nosy aunts rolled up into one. "It was fine." She sent Nora what she hoped was a benign smile and got herself a glass of water. Nora waved off Kate's offer of one.

"You know, I can't understand why someone would want to spend his life living out of a suitcase. Obviously, he has no clue about settling down. Women like you need the stable types, like my Niles. Which brings me to the real reason I'm here. Did Tyler buy stuff to fix your windows?"

"I don't think so," Kate said.

Nora crossed her arms. "Didn't figure he'd remember that. All his words were just for show. I'll have Niles get some of those safety pins. Can't be too careful, you know. He's arriving earlier than planned. The twenty-first. Are you free?"

Kate reached into her purse for her calendar. Flipping it open, she saw that the next two weekends were depressingly empty if you didn't count the office Christmas party. Her last classes would be over by Thursday, and after that, the university was on winter break. "I've got the firm's annual holiday party, but I'm pretty available."

"Good. I'll touch base with Niles and be back with you. Now, it's getting late. I can't survive without my beauty sleep. You, however, look as lovely as always. Don't forget to lock up behind me."

"I won't." Kate waited until Nora was out the door before slumping against it. She still had to tell Nora she didn't want to go on a date with Niles. Kate sighed. She was sure that once she met him he wouldn't be interested in her anyway, and probably was just as tired of his grandmother's matchmaking as Kate was.

Although, in the spirit of Christmas and if she could survive one date with the sexy Tyler Nichols, Kate could easily survive Niles, especially with Nora there to chaperone.

Another knock sounded, and Kate groaned. She paused before she turned the dead bolt and threw open the door. "What did you forget, Nora?"

"Nothing and I'm not Nora," a husky voice said. Kate dropped her hand to her side and stared at Tyler. He gave her a tentative smile. "Mind if I come in?"

"No. Of course not. Forgive my bad manners." Kate moved aside and gestured him in. She walked over to the kitchen sink and leaned against the counter. "Is everything okay?"

Tyler nodded. "Yeah. No problem. I thought it would be best if we exchanged information, and the sooner the better. Phone numbers, keys, things like that."

"Keys?" Kate frowned. Why did he want to swap keys?

"Yes," Tyler confirmed. "I'd like to give you mine, and ask if you'd retrieve my mail from the curb for the next two weeks. I'm leaving tomorrow for California to do a piece on Arnold as governor."

"Oh." Kate snatched at composure. He'd just moved in and now he was vanishing. Raw disappointment filled her. She'd known he wasn't the type to stay around long. Why had she hoped otherwise? "Of course I'll get your mail."

It was, after all, the neighborly thing to do.

"Here's my business card." Tyler put it in her hand and her palm warmed where his fingers grazed hers. "My work number and e-mail address are on it, and I've written my parents' number and my cell phone on the back. I've got voice mail on the cell phone, so don't hesitate to leave a message if I don't answer. Because I'm often gone, I use a financial service, so don't worry if you don't see any bills. Just leave whatever I get on the kitchen table. My sister will check in on occasion, but not too often, since it's a pretty far drive—she lives on the other side of town. Here. Write your number on the back of this."

Tyler handed Kate another of his business cards. She picked up a pen and jotted down her work and home phone numbers on the card, then handed it over. Swapping phone numbers seemed so personal, yet the act was really nothing more than something neighbors did.

"Don't worry about anything while you're gone. I'll be happy to look after your house and make sure no newspapers pile up. It's something we do on Dogwood Lane. We watch out for one another," she said, her impartial tone indicating that it was no big deal.

"Ah. Neighborhood Watch." Tyler took the card and studied Kate's numbers for a moment.

"Exactly. We do it for everybody." There. That sounded good, Kate decided. Less exclusive and more impersonal. Still, she stepped away from his magnetic proximity as he moved closer to set his key on the kitchen table.

Tyler read the card again. "Your work number seems familiar." He shrugged and put the card in his pocket. "So how's studying going?"

"Okay, I guess. I was enjoying a short break when Nora came over. She wanted to check that you'd gotten the things for my windows."

Tyler winced. "I knew there was something we forgot when we were out. I'll take care of it when I get back."

"That's fine. Niles can do it. Nora's arranging it."

"I don't want you doing anything with Niles," Tyler growled. He ran his fingers through his hair. Curly locks straightened and then recurled.

"It's nothing," Kate said. "I'm no more interested in him than I am you."

Tyler eyed her for a long moment before speaking. "I'll be in California doing a follow-up on Arnold being governor."

"You said that," she pointed out.

"I just wanted to make sure you remembered." Tyler strode across the floor toward her, and Kate's stomach flipped. He stood less than a foot from her, invading her personal space, but instead of minding, she wished he were even closer. His eyes darkened to a glistening brown and Kate's mouth opened slightly. The fullness of his lips, the cleft of his chin and the one sexily askew eyelash were incredibly alluring.

As if sensing the chemistry between them, Tyler lifted her jaw with his finger, making their lips now only a scant distance apart.

"I just wanted you to be sure you had your story right for work tomorrow. I'd hate to have you stumble if you decide to go through with this plan of yours, especially when you aren't really interested in me."

Kate nodded, her gaze locked on his. She didn't care about the stupid plan of hers. "California. Governor. I've got it."

"Good." Tyler ran his finger lightly down her throat, stopping when he reached her collarbone. Kate swallowed, her mouth suddenly dry. Tyler continued to hold her gaze. "So, you aren't interested in me?"

"No," Kate whispered, voicing a lie.

He recognized the untruth, as well, for all of a sudden he brought his mouth down. His lips were demanding, and Kate sighed and leaned into him as the heat flared. His body was hard and solid, and Kate didn't protest as he lifted her arms and placed them around his neck. She wanted this. Had from the moment she'd first seen him outside her kitchen door, if that was possible. Once again, she wondered how she could be so connected to someone she didn't really know, but as he slid his arms around her back, she decided she didn't care.

She wasn't a cold fish. This was passion. Pure. Un-adulterated. She wasn't frigid. Far from it.

Tyler tugged at her tucked-in shirt, and Kate shivered uncontrollably as his tongue touched hers. Tomorrow, she'd worry about the consequences. Right now, for the first time in her life, Kate was simply going to let herself feel what she'd been missing, let him confirm that she wasn't a passionless freak of nature.

"Tyler." She murmured his name against his mouth, and he groaned in return. Kate's world had spun on its axis too fast, and the air hissed as Tyler lifted her shirt free from the confining waistband—

Wait. The air wasn't hissing. The thought intruded through the haze of pleasure too late as sharp claws dug through her socks, causing her to shriek. She jerked her leg out of the cat's reach, kicking out and colliding with Tyler's knee as she did so.

Tyler lost his balance. "Ouch!"

"Sorry!" Kate bit back curse words as the cat disappeared into another room. "Jeckyll just scratched me!"

Tyler somehow steadied them and lowered Kate onto a kitchen chair. He bent on his knee and pulled her anklet down, then gently touched her foot. Kate's flesh quivered. Tyler replaced her sock and stood. "The scratch wasn't too deep."

"Good," Kate said. She was a little shaken and her breathing was shallow—reactions to both Jeckyll's attack and the fact that she'd been kissing Tyler.

"I think you've got a jealous cat," Tyler observed.

"Either that or a hungry one," Kate replied, regaining some composure. "His food bowl is empty. He can get extremely cranky when he's too hungry."

"If nothing else, he's a good chaperone. It's probably best we stopped. But I enjoyed kissing you. A lot." She could read the truth in his eyes as he placed a finger on her puffy lips, causing them to tingle. "We both should get some rest tonight. I'm flying across the country tomorrow and you probably have to get back to studying. While I want this, now is probably not the best time."

"I'll keep an eye on your house." The words seemed so banal after what had just happened. Kate rested against the chair, grateful she had something propping her up.

"Thank you." Tyler's voice was soft. Kate wasn't sure what he was thanking her for—watching his house or responding to his kiss. He moved away and opened the kitchen door. He stepped out, then stepped back in partially and gazed at her.

"Kate," he called.

"Yes?" Kate's voice came out a hoarse whisper, but Tyler didn't seem to notice.

"I want you to remember one thing while I'm gone."

"I'll get the mail and won't worry if I don't see any bills." Kate gave him a smile, one he didn't return. He looked so intense.

He shook his head. "No, that's not it."
A lump formed in her throat. "Oh. Then what?"
"I'm not a myth." And with that, he was gone.

Chapter Eight

"You know, if I wasn't so hungover from three nights of partying, I'd probably still be mad at you," Wendy said early Monday morning as she stopped by Kate's cubicle on her way to the photocopier. "Lucky for me my boss is in court all day today, so I don't have to face him until late this afternoon."

"Yeah, lucky for you. I, however, am not as fortunate." Kate gestured to the six-inch stack of file folders on her desk. "Marshall's on a tear. He's doing depositions at the end of the week for the Tierney case. I have a lot of prep to do to get him ready."

"You can start in a few minutes. All I know is that you may not be lucky at work, but from what I saw Friday night, I'd say you got lucky this weekend. I want the details. When I left here, I thought we were going out. Although if I were in a bedroom with that hunk, I probably wouldn't surface, either. So spill the beans. Who is he?"

Kate blushed. "I've already told you. He's my new neighbor."

Wendy's mouth formed an O, her expression incredulous. "Really? I thought everyone on your block had one foot in the grave."

"They do not. Anyway, he just moved in. Myra's children left the place a mess and I was helping him clean."

"I'd say you were helping him. I'd clean him any day." Wendy ignored the roll of Kate's eyes. "Did you see his biceps?" Wendy giggled. "Oops. I'd say you did more than see them. I guess if you were going to break your dry spell, he was the way to do it."

Yes, Kate had felt those biceps. Maybe not quite in the way Wendy meant, but Kate had caressed every taut muscle on Tyler's arm during their embrace in her kitchen. Unable to figure out how to answer, Kate stayed silent.

"I admit to being jealous. Not one man at the party was worth his salt. I bet your neighbor was incredible. All I met this weekend were losers. But not you. No, you finally followed my advice. I always knew you had a secret wild side under those frumpy clothes."

"There is nothing wrong with my clothes," Kate protested. Unlike many of the women in the office, who wore upscale, fashionable work attire, Kate dressed plainly for expediency's sake. She kept her hair in a bun for the same reason. Even though the law offices were in the suburbs—"the largest firm in Orlando and we're not even downtown," her boss would brag—she hated to get up any earlier than necessary, and slept in until the last possible second, especially since she only averaged five to six hours of sleep a night. Not curling her hair and leaving it down gave her an extra fifteen minutes of snooze time. Kate wasn't vain about her looks. She took the extra sleep. Once she became a full-fledged lawyer, she'd have to dress to the nines at all times. But by then she'd be finished with school and could go to bed earlier.

"So," Wendy said as she moved the file folders aside. "What's lover boy's name? What does he do? Is he good?"

Kate averted her gaze to hide her guilt. She knew Wendy wasn't talking about Tyler's work. But his kisses *were* good, although that was a secret she was keeping to herself.

"His name is Tyler Nichols and he's a photojournalist."

"A photojournalist." Wendy sighed. "So glamorous."

Kate used to think that, but now she knew better. From Tyler's description, living in a leaky tent on a front line didn't sound very glamorous.

"So, what station does he work for?"

"Huh?" Kate looked at Wendy. "Oh, he works for a wire service."

"Cool. So when will you see him again?"

Kate suddenly understood the reason Tyler had insisted that she learn his itinerary. She'd have to thank him for his foresight. "I'm not sure. He's on assignment in California. He said it could take up to two weeks. He gave me a key to his house."

"He gave you a key?" Wendy parroted. Her eyes narrowed. "When?"

Kate crossed her fingers behind her back. She hadn't expected such scrutiny. The only positive was that thus far Kate hadn't told any outright, huge lies. Actually, a lot of what she was saying was the truth. Just selectively featured, as on reality TV. "He gave me a key last night after we went out to eat."

"So there was more than just that night?" Wendy practically squeaked the word. "I'm thrilled. You really must have made an impression on him."

"Well…" Kate let the word trail off. If she said anything else, she'd dig herself a big hole.

"So where did he take you?" Wendy frowned as she noticed she'd chipped a nail.

"Just out for a late lunch."

"Wait until I tell the girls. They'll die. We've been hoping you'd find someone."

Kate's phone beeped and the intercom came on. "Kate?" her boss, Marshall Evans, said.

Kate pressed the button so that the call turned two-way. "Yes?"

"I need you in here. Bring in the Adams-Counts file."

"On my way." Kate released the button.

Wendy stood. "Meet me at noon, downstairs by the statue. Today's Monday. That means Eve's roast-beef-sandwich special. Don't be late. You know how the crowd gets."

All the girls in the office had become addicted to Eve's roast beef. On Mondays the place was jammed with customers.

"I'll be there," Kate replied as she grabbed the file folder and headed toward her boss's office.

The morning flew by, as did lunch.

"So can you believe the news about Theresa?" Wendy asked as she and Kate rode the elevator back upstairs. "She's finally engaged."

"I'm so happy for her," Kate said. *And relieved for myself,* she thought. Conversation had focused on Theresa's nuptials, not Kate's date.

"I want to be married someday," Wendy sighed as they walked out of the elevator and onto Kate's floor. "Don't you?"

"I suppose," Kate said. "Don't we all want that? But I'm not trying to find someone."

"No, because you already have," Wendy said. "I mean, I like running through all my Mr. Right Nows. But eventually I'd like to find that perfect man and settle down. Hey. What are those?"

"What?" Kate stepped forward. There were flowers waiting in Kate's cubicle. Not just any flowers. Upon tearing the paper, Kate discovered twelve long-stemmed pink roses.

"Those are gorgeous! Did Tyler send them?" Wendy, still with Kate, fingered one of the bright pink petals.

Kate's hand trembled as she reached for the card. "I don't know. No one's ever sent me flowers." The fragrance of the blooms permeated Kate's space.

"It has to be Tyler. Quick. Open the card."

Kate gingerly removed the small envelope from its plastic-pitchfork holder. She touched the envelope for a moment before she slid her forefinger under the flap and ripped the seam open.

"What's it say?" Wendy asked, her curiosity getting the best of her. She peeked around Kate's shoulder.

Kate read the card, realizing the handwriting was probably the florist's. "It says, 'Kate, I hope this helps. I am not a myth. Tyler.'"

"Wow," Wendy said before glancing at her watch. She grimaced as she noted the time.

Kate didn't answer but instead fingered one of the rose petals. The pink bloom was silky soft and delightful to the touch.

"Kate? I've got to go. I'll e-mail you. Wait until everyone hears about this."

"Great," Kate mumbled, not paying much attention

to Wendy's departure. Instead, she just stood there, in dazed but glorious shock, staring at the flowers in front of her.

Tyler had sent her roses. She felt another petal, as if reassuring herself the flowers weren't an illusion. And he'd written that he wasn't a myth.

The sleeplessness that his kiss had produced proved his point.

He was a desirable man. But, as she had acknowledged to herself so many times already, she wanted permanence. Nine to five. Monday through Friday. Tyler was working in California. Who knew where he'd go next? Kate swallowed and tried to focus on work. Maybe she should call him. Tell him that his gift was too much, way over the top. She pulled his business card out of her purse. She dialed before she would lose her nerve, but when his voice mail answered, she changed her mind and hung up. She'd give herself the day to create a plan of action.

She'd made this mess; she'd deal with it. Gossip died down. Her life was not exciting enough for the girls in the office to dwell on it too long. This would pass, as would Tyler's interest.

By Thursday afternoon, she still hadn't contacted Tyler or decided what to do about him. However, the situation at work seemed to have resolved itself. Although most of the female coworkers she socialized with had stopped by her cubicle to see her flowers, to Kate's relief not one of her friends pressed her about Tyler or his plans. Predictably, most of the week's lunch discussions centered on Theresa and what type of wedding she wanted.

Kate finished up the legal brief she'd been typing

and realized that she'd never gotten so much studying or work done. She placed the last file in her out-box and leaned back, satisfied with herself. For a moment she was caught up—well, until Marshall finished his emergency conference with one of the partners and gave her another task.

Kate took a moment to check her work e-mail, then her personal e-mail. She'd sent Tyler a thank-you e-mail, but he hadn't replied.

One of her school peers had e-mailed her some lecture notes and Kate used the free time to study for her final that night. By the time a shadow fell across her desk, she had almost finished reading.

"Hi," an unfamiliar female voice said.

Startled, Kate jerked upright. A pretty blonde stood at her cubicle. While Kate didn't know the woman personally, she recognized her as Tara McCabe, one of the junior partners.

Disconcerted, Kate belatedly remembered her manners. "May I help you?"

The woman blinked, her perusal of Kate finished. "I've come to see your flowers."

Considering partners didn't socialize with the paralegals, that was odd, but Kate simply scooted her chair over. Ms. McCabe strode over to the flowers. "They're beautiful."

"Thank you." Kate knew that within the next few days the roses would begin to wilt. She dreaded that. She'd grown quite fond of them.

"I heard they were from some photojournalist. Tyler something. Is his last name Nichols?" Tara asked.

Kate nodded mutely as her stomach churned. Could Tyler have once been dating someone who worked at her firm? He'd given no indication of knowing anyone there—wait, he'd said her work number looked familiar. Was that how he'd known where to send the flowers? She'd been so enamored of the roses that now she couldn't remember if she'd ever told Tyler the name of her employer.

"I guess we need to talk. Do you mind if I sit down? When I overheard my paralegal mention the name Tyler Nichols, I had to find out if it was the very same Tyler I know."

"I—I just met him," Kate sputtered. Maybe she should have taken his six-degrees-of-separation warning more seriously.

"He was only home for the weekend before he left for California." The woman shook her head and a blond hair fell askew. "You must be the neighbor he and Jamie were fighting over."

How did Tara know about that? Kate was out of her depth.

"It's too small a world," Tara went on.

The intercom buzzed, and grateful for the diversion, Kate answered it. Marshall's voice shot out from the handset. "Is Tara McCabe with you?"

"Yes," Kate replied.

"Let me talk to her."

"Just a moment." Kate switched off the speaker and passed the phone over to Tara.

Tara listened for a moment. "Okay, Marshall. I'll be right in." She held out the phone and Kate returned it to its cradle. "Listen, I'm in court tomorrow, but would you like to have lunch with me Saturday? I'm going to check on Tyler's house, so I'll be in the neighborhood. I'll stop by—say, about noonish."

Without waiting for an answer, Tara left the cubicle. Kate stared after her, dread lining her stomach. Just what had she gotten herself into?

Chapter Nine

On Friday morning, Tyler took one last glance around his hotel room. He'd packed all his clothes, and his camera bag was on his shoulder. "That's everything," he told the bellhop, who would store his luggage until that afternoon when the crew would pick it up and head to the airport for the next part of their trip.

The pace had been intense, but they'd managed to get the work done. Only one more week and then he could go home.

Home. He frowned as he followed the bellhop from the room. He usually described finishing a job as "ready for a break." Not "going home."

Had Dogwood Lane already become home? Sure, he'd never owned a house, but putting down some roots didn't mean anything.

Tyler stepped into the elevator and punched the button for the lobby. The fact that Kate hadn't called bothered him. He'd expected to hear from her, found himself waiting for contact. They'd had such a great time on their date. Kate's presence had made the shopping trip special. He liked her and enjoyed being with her. He'd experienced a spark of something special.

But he was pretty certain she didn't feel the same, and obviously, his flowers hadn't done the job.

His cell phone was working. Others had left him messages, but not Kate. She hadn't e-mailed, either. Then again, the corporate spam blocker could have eaten any e-mail. That happened frequently.

Weren't flowers worth a phone call? He never sent women flowers, but he'd assumed a thank-you phone call was the proper response to them. Heck, Kate hadn't even phoned to tell him his house was fine. Wasn't that what neighbors did?

He wanted to talk to her, but he knew it was tacky to call up and ask, "Did you get my flowers?"

Although…he did know one guy who had sent roses and then discovered that in the rush of Valentine's Day the store hadn't delivered them. That it really had been the store's fault was the only thing that had kept the guy out of the doghouse.

Tyler reached the lobby. His colleagues were gathering by the doors. Darn it all. He was a photojournalist on the other side of the country, a man without staying power, who was only in Kate's life so that everyone would stop playing matchmaker. What was that about wanting what he couldn't have? Perhaps he should just respect her wishes. After all, his job was his calling. He loved the rush of a story, the adrenaline of getting the perfect shot.

He glanced at his coworkers and then at his watch. Florida was on eastern standard time, three hours ahead of California, and his group still had a few people missing. Tyler pulled out his cell phone and dialed.

"Hey, sis," he said when Tara answered.

"Tyler! Good to hear from you but bad timing. I'm

due back in court in five minutes. You caught me in the middle of a short recess."

"Guess I'm lucky that way." Tyler grinned. His sister always cheered him up.

"I'd say so. You sent flowers!"

He didn't think he'd heard her right and he frowned. "I didn't send you any flowers."

"Not me. Kate. You sent Kate Merrill flowers. I saw them myself. Your name's been on the tip of all the paralegals' tongues this week. Your neighbor works at my office!"

"Yeah, I figured that out." Tyler shifted the phone to the other ear so he could run his free hand through his hair. He'd risked Tara's finding this out when he'd spoken with the florist, but he'd thought the greater good was more important. However, his plan for Kate to phone him and consider him more than a friend had backfired.

"Tyler, I felt so stupid. You could have told me about her before you left. She's probably thinking I'm some sort of nutcase the way I descended on her in her cubicle."

"Tara—" Tyler began, but his sister cut him off.

"Anyway, I could tell you really liked her, so I told Mom. I'm taking her to lunch tomorrow."

"You're what?" His throat constricted.

"I said I'm taking her to lunch." Tara spoke louder, as if the connection was poor and she wanted to make sure he heard her. "If you're serious about her, then I'd like to get to know her. It's not like you introduced us the other night. Besides, didn't you say she was studying law? That means we have a lot in common. You must be serious if you sent flowers. I know you. I mean, you are serious, aren't you? You'd tell me if you weren't."

Suddenly, Tyler was at a loss for words. He contemplated the situation. He should reveal the truth—that he and Kate weren't really dating. Then again, he couldn't blow Kate's cover. "Were they pretty?" he asked.

"They were perfect. Beautiful. She loved them."

Tyler watched the rest of the crew arrive. From across the lobby they eyed him expectantly, and he held up a finger, asking for another minute. "Tara, listen, I need to tell you—"

"Don't backpedal now. If the grapevine is correct, you and Kate have really hit it off. 'Spontaneous combustion that flared into fantastic sex' is how I heard it described. Anyway, Mom's ecstatic that you're seeing someone. It'll keep her from worrying. We'll talk when you get back. Break's over. Ciao."

"Tara!" Tyler realized he was shouting into empty space. His sister had already disconnected. Damn. This was not good. He yanked angrily on his collar.

His mother now thought he was dating someone. She'd be on him double-time to settle down. His sister was also relentless, was more so when she thought she was helping out. And, of course, the last thing Tyler wanted his family to be discussing was his sex life, especially the fantastic sex everyone but him had been privy to!

But the real kicker was that Kate had received his flowers. And said nothing.

"Ready?" Luke asked as Tyler approached.

"Yeah," Tyler said. He followed everyone outside to where transportation waited. As he climbed into the van, Tyler flipped his phone back open. He punched speed dial. After the phone clicked a few times, another female finally answered.

"Jess." Tyler calmed his breathing. "Darling, we've got to talk. I'm going to need a little time off."

AT ELEVEN-THIRTY Saturday morning, Kate removed the one letter she found in Tyler's mailbox. From the return address, she could tell that already the junk-mail distributors had found him. That hadn't taken long, Kate mused.

She closed the black box and, seeing Nora, gave her a quick wave. Nora, busy adjusting her inflatable Santa Claus, briefly waved back, and Kate turned and walked up the driveway. Even though she was sure Tyler would probably trash the offer for the dating service, she still put the flyer on the kitchen table. Tyler didn't seem like a man who would require dating help.

Kate read the flyer. The company promised to find your perfect match. She smiled. She'd managed to reach the eighth of December without one offer of being fixed up. That had to be a record.

Tyler had all his Christmas lights on a timer, so that was one thing Kate hadn't worried about. Kate locked up and exited just as a zippy red sports car pulled up under the carport.

"Hi, Kate!" Tara got out of her car, impeccably dressed in designer jeans, a white silk shirt and navy blue blazer. "How's it going?"

"Fine," Kate said. "I just put the mail on the table."

"So the house is okay?" Tara used her key and took a moment to check for herself. Kate followed her back into Tyler's kitchen. "Look's great. Thanks for doing such a good job. Ready for lunch? I thought we'd go to this bistro I know. I met a client there and that's how I found this neighborhood."

"Look, uh, Ms. McCabe..."

"Tara," she corrected.

"Tara. I don't think this is such a good idea."

She appeared stunned. "Why not? Tyler would want us to get to know each other. He indicated as much when I talked to him yesterday. I still can't believe he didn't tell me about the flowers himself, but that's how he is. He gets tunnel vision when he's working. Anyway, I told him we were going to lunch and he didn't object."

"Um, this is awkward. I mean, whatever your relationship is with Tyler..."

"Relationship?" Tara blinked rapidly, as if she was confused. "I've known Tyler all my life. Since the womb. Oh. You thought..." Tara laughed.

"Really, I—" Kate began.

"Oh, Kate, it's okay. I get it. Since my last name is different, you thought I was..." She laughed again and put out her hand. "Let's start over. Hi, Kate, I'm Tara Nichols McCabe. Tyler's twin sister."

"Nice to meet you. I guess." Kate experienced overpowering relief as she returned Tara's handshake.

"It will be now that we've cleared all that up," Tara said with a laugh. "Let's do lunch. I'm starving."

"Me, too. I have to admit I was imagining the worst."

The lines around Tara's eyes crinkled. "It's fine, really. Do you need your purse?"

"Yes, and I need to lock my house up, now that my nerves are subsiding." Kate took a deep breath. She'd been nervous and even a little jealous. Okay, a lot jealous. She'd declared Tyler just a guy to help her out, but since his kiss and the flowers, she simply couldn't think of him platonically anymore.

"What's this? Divorce law?" Tara said, spying Kate's textbook on the kitchen table once they were in Kate's house.

"I'm studying to be a lawyer. I graduate in May."

"I heard you were in school." Tara opened the book. "Does Marshall know about this?"

"Yes. I felt it only ethical to tell him. He's offered me a job, but I'm not sure if I want to start off in such a large firm. I was thinking something smaller might be better."

"Keep me posted on your decision," Tara said. "I'm interested, and not just because you're dating my brother. Everyone deserves a break now and then, and if Marshall's offered you a spot, that's huge. Marshall doesn't say things he doesn't mean, and he wouldn't make any offer unless he's serious."

"You're probably right," Kate said, a bit in awe of her good fortune. While she'd worked for Marshall for years, she'd simply rationalized his offer as one of politeness.

Tara laughed. "I am right. Well, maybe not in all things."

At the bistro Kate found herself enjoying both the lunch and Tara's company. Tyler's twin was witty, and she hadn't been embarrassed in the slightest to tell Kate about her "quickie Vegas marriage and quickie divorce."

"Tyler was furious," she said. "He railed at me for a month even after the divorce papers were finalized. Trust me, what goes on in Vegas doesn't always stay there."

"You were young," Kate said.

"Yeah, newly twenty-one and a little too toasty on champagne. I was trying to do the right thing and not have a one-night stand with the brother of one of my best friends, whom I'd had a crush on for years. So I made him marry me first. What was I thinking? I wanted out the very next morning and so did he."

"Yet you kept his name."

"A bit of protection. People look at you differently when you've been married. In a sense, it's made my career run smoother. People perceive an older single woman as desperate, as if they're afraid that she has some ticking biological clock on her."

"Tell me about it," Kate said.

"Oh, I know. Our office is terrible. I overhear the paralegals talk. The place is like blind-date city."

"The girls do like to fix everyone up," Kate admitted.

"Which is why I kept my married name. A divorced person is perceived as once bitten, twice shy. I can focus on my career without people worrying I'm on a constant manhunt."

Kate could understand that. She'd used Tyler for the very same reason. "I'm just trying to finish school," Kate said.

"Does Tyler know your goals? You've definitely captured his interest. I was there the day the appliances were installed—the day you canceled the date. He wasn't happy."

"Really, we aren't that serious," Kate said.

"You may not be, but I think he is. You've got staying power, and perhaps you'll do my brother a world of good. Tyler needs to get some grass growing under his feet." Tara sipped her coffee. "So have you asked him to the company Christmas party next weekend?"

That was next Saturday, and Kate hadn't planned on attending the annual event. "I usually don't go. I'm not a huge fan of social scenes like that."

"You should take Tyler," Tara said. "Marshall's met my brother and likes him. Since Marshall's already offered you a spot when you graduate, that means he's impressed with you. Even if you choose to work elsewhere, think of the party as a chance to hone your schmoozing skills and gain a good recommendation."

Tara was probably right. Of course, a side benefit was that everyone would meet Tyler. But was perpetuating the charade a wise idea? Doing so could suck her in further, making it impossible to end the farce without hurting everyone's feelings and/or making herself look bad. Sandra had always said honesty was the best policy. Why hadn't Kate learned that yet?

Tara glanced across the rim of her white porcelain cup. "Say yes."

Kate forced a light laugh. "I'll ask Tyler. If he agrees, then I'll go."

Tara's lips turned upward. "Good try. Trust me, you won't get a chance to use that escape clause. Tyler will go. So what type of law do you want to specialize in?"

Kate was grateful that Tara had changed the subject. Being with Tyler twisted her stomach into knots and made her want what she'd long ago disavowed. "I like family law best. Adoptions and things like that." Kate sipped her water. She'd always planned to help those less fortunate.

Tara nodded her approval. "An area I didn't ever desire to do. You know, I'm glad we met. I'm sure we'll be seeing quite a lot of each other now that you're dating my brother."

Guilt bore down on Kate. The reality was that she'd created an elaborate hoax that minute by minute spiraled more and more out of control. Sure, she found Tyler sexy. He'd kissed her and she'd liked it. He'd given her a key to his house. He'd sent flowers. But a relationship? Hardly. So Kate simply smiled and enjoyed the rest of her time out before going home to study.

She'd been at it a few hours when she heard a knock on her door. Slowly, she pushed the curtains aside and peered out, winning a nod of approval from Nora, who stood on the other side. "Hi, Kate! I made a pot roast, and there's no way I can eat it all. Have you eaten?" Nora held up plastic storage containers as she entered the kitchen.

"I had lunch with Tyler's sister. We work at the same law firm." Kate closed the door behind Nora.

"She's the blonde with the sports car I saw in his driveway earlier?" Nora bustled about Kate's kitchen, stepping past Jeckyll with a "Shoo. None for you" as she put the containers in the refrigerator.

"That's her," Kate confirmed.

"Tara," Nora said, committing the name to memory.

"Yes," Kate confirmed.

"Tyler told me she'd be watching his house on occasion. So you two work together."

"Yes. She's a junior partner at the firm. I didn't know because her last name is different from Tyler's," Kate said.

"Such a small world after all," Nora quipped.

"Uh-huh," Kate said, starting to be concerned about to where Nora was directing the conversation.

Nora leaned against the refrigerator and waited a second or two before saying, "So does she believe you're really dating her brother?"

Kate folded her hands. "Yes. Tyler sent me flowers."

"You've woven a twisted web," Nora said. "I over-heard you talking that night and wondered what you were scheming. Tyler's not in your league, Kate. He's a man who's traveled the world. I'm worried you're going to get hurt."

"Well, what if I like him?" Kate said.

"I like George Clooney, but that doesn't mean I could keep his interest," Nora said matter-of-factly. "Tyler's like a jet-setter. You're a…" She paused as she searched for the right word. "You're the settling kind, Kate. That's not Tyler. I promised Sandra I'd watch out for you. I only want what's best for you."

"And I thank you for that. You know how much that means to me. But I can handle this. It'll be fine," Kate said, even if she wasn't exactly sure herself. Her web of lies was big.

"If you're sure," Nora said. "I'm always here for you."

"I know," Kate said. "I've made some poor choices in the past, but Tyler and I aren't serious. We're just hav-ing fun. I deserve that."

"You do," Nora agreed. "You've worked so hard. San-dra would be very proud. I know I am. You're within reach of all your goals. I'm just afraid you'll be side-tracked by wanting something you can't have."

"All I want is for people to leave me alone. There's nothing wrong with being single. Lots of women are. I have a full life. I don't need to add a man to the mix. Hence, Tyler. He's perfect. He's never around."

"Kate, you deserve the best. You deserve it all—to have a love like the one I had, like Frieda had. Sure she can be annoying sometimes, but we're united in this one. You shouldn't settle."

"I'm not planning on settling," Kate insisted. "I can handle this—" she thought a moment "—thing with Tyler. Maybe it's time I let everything play out."

"What about Niles?" Nora asked. "He's still interested in meeting you."

"As long as you don't take it personally if we don't hit it off," Kate said. "I love you, Nora, but I'm ready to handle this relationship stuff myself for a while. Even if that means mucking it up along the way. I'm ready for that. No more matchmaking."

Nora nodded, and a satisfied smile broke out on her face. "Okay, I agree. I believe you are ready, Kate. Just as long as you understand that I'm still going to meddle a little. I don't think I could ever stop. I'm set in my ways and leopards can't change their spots. So dinner with Niles?"

"Maybe. But just dinner. Nothing more," Kate said.

"Good. Speaking of dinner, don't forget to heat that pot roast the old-fashioned way, using a three-fifty oven for twenty minutes. If you microwave it, it just doesn't turn out right. Dries the meat out and makes it too chewy."

"Okay," Kate said. "I can manage it."

"Well, I'm off. The seniors' center is having its annual Christmas party tonight. Don't forget to lock up tight, especially if you're not going anywhere."

"I won't. I'll be Christmas-shopping next week, since I'll be finished with finals. I've taken a few and have just a couple others." Nora left, and Kate closed the door and clicked the lock. She exhaled. Well, that conversation had gone a lot smoother than she'd expected, especially as unplanned as it was. Maybe things were finally turning in her direction.

TYLER REALLY shouldn't have driven home from the airport. It had been a stupid move on his part, but it was too late to turn back now. At least he was home.

He'd never thought of any of his apartments as more than places to store his stuff. Somehow Dogwood Lane had seeped into his blood. Or maybe Kate had. Maybe that was it. He'd never asked his assignment editor for what he'd asked Friday. The moment his replacement had arrived Saturday afternoon, Tyler had been on the first flight home, a red-eye that had arrived at 5:00 a.m. He'd been unable to sleep on the plane, probably the only passenger on the packed flight not zoned out and catching z's.

Tyler rolled down the window and let the cool December breeze rush in. Only two more streets to go. Finally, his driveway crunched under the Hummer's tires, and Tyler brought the vehicle to a stop under his darkened carport.

He felt like a zombie.

He probably looked like one, too. He'd been on the go since five yesterday morning, so he'd been up over twenty-four hours. He stepped out of the car and went to the house. In the dark he couldn't see which key unlocked the side door. After trying every one, including the car key both right side up and upside down, Tyler gave up. Whatever key he had, it didn't work. He frowned. Why didn't he have the right key?

Of course. He'd given it to Kate. And his spare was inside in his den. He'd had a feeling he'd forgotten to do something at the hardware store before he'd rushed off to the airport. Now he knew what.

Presented with two choices, Tyler chose the lesser of two evils. Rather than face Nora and the local police if he tried to break in, he went over to Kate's kitchen door and started knocking.

A lamp flicked on, and Tyler blinked as the light assaulted his eyes. He shielded them as the light for Kate's carport flew on.

She stared at him. "Tyler? You aren't supposed to be back yet, are you? What are you doing here?"

"You have my key." Tyler heard the welcome sound of locks clicking open.

"Well, get in here before Nora wakes up and calls the cops."

Still shading his eyes, Tyler entered Kate's kitchen. Already she was turning off extra lights and bringing his surroundings back into a less painful perspective. He slumped onto a kitchen chair.

Tyler removed his hands from his eyes to find Kate standing in front of him. "Thanks for letting me in. I didn't feel like explaining to the police why I broke a window. I figured if I got caught, I'd never live it down."

"No, you wouldn't. The gossips on this street would talk about you for months." Kate peered at him. "Hey, are you okay? You look terrible."

"Probably. I've been up for more than twenty-four hours. I'm ready to sleep for days. Except…"

Kate glanced down. Her robe had gaped. "Do you always look this good so early in the morning?" he asked.

"Um, no. And it's dawn. Sun's coming up. Church in a few hours." She pulled her robe shut. "You, however, need sleep. Go home and get to bed. Let me grab your key."

"Bed sounds good," he replied, closing his eyes to shut off the vision of Kate's retreating backside.

"Tyler, I've got your key," Kate said as she reentered the room less than a minute later. Tyler's head rested on her kitchen table and Jeckyll had curled up around him. Her next-door neighbor was out.

She touched him gently on the shoulder. "Tyler?"

"What?" His head shot up, his fast reaction causing Kate to jump back. "I'm awake," he said quickly.

She watched him, fascinated. "I've got your key."

The adrenaline wore off when he realized he wasn't in danger. "How about I just stay right here and sleep?" he mumbled. "I don't need a bed."

"Yes, but what would the neighbors think?"

He grew sleepier, and his husky tone tickled her ear. "I'm a neighbor. I think it's fine."

She left him there a moment until common sense ruled. "Tyler! You cannot sleep at my table."

Tyler raised his head again, his expression sheepish. "Yeah, okay."

He rose to his feet, his sleepiness vanishing. His eyes darkened as he gazed at her. Kate knew she was powerless to resist the truth—she wanted this man the way she'd wanted no other and darn the consequences. He'd tempted her all week and he hadn't even been in the same state.

"You're right about the table," he said, lowering his mouth to hers as if he, too, had known kissing her was inevitable. "Your bed would be much more comfortable."

His mouth was hot and heavy and she molded to him

as the kiss deepened. Kate arched her neck and Tyler lowered his lips to the hollow at the base of her throat.

"I want to make love to you," he said without pretense. No fancy words, no false declarations. Just what he intended. Lost to the sensations he was drawing from her, Kate could only nod her assent.

"I thought of you this week," he said, sliding his lips down to the vee of her robe. His fingers were untying the belt at her waist, and he pushed the flannel garment back from her shoulders but not off.

"Not lace, but close enough," he said before he nuzzled her right breast through the silk cami top. His left hand looped under her buttocks, lifting her to meet him. Crushed against him, Kate experienced every bit of his arousal and longing shot through her. Tyler sat her on the kitchen table. "You didn't call," he told her.

"I e-mailed."

"Uh-huh."

His fingers were everywhere, heating her flesh anywhere he touched. He slid the cami straps down and replaced his fingers with his mouth. Then he dropped lower. Surely he wasn't going to... His fingers moved under her boxers, pushing the fabric aside. Kate detonated at the first touch of his lips. "I knew it." Tyler murmured against the inside of her thigh. "So hot."

She was hot.

She shuddered with pleasure and with the joy of realization. Jack the Jerk had called her frigid; the beautiful and gorgeous Tyler Nichols had called her hot. She could only let herself go as her release carried her away.

And then he kissed her mouth, gathering her semi-naked body to his. "Bed," he said, cradling her to him.

"Bed," she repeated, linking her arms around his neck.

But just then, far away in the bedroom, Kate's alarm clock shrilled, shattering the moment. The microwave read seven-fifteen.

"I can't," Kate whispered as the moment ended. "I'm taking Frieda to church. Her new glasses had to be repaired already and she can't drive without them."

The air hung heavy as the magic of the interlude faded. "I should probably go," Tyler said.

Kate drew her robe around her. "You need sleep. This was a—"

"Don't say this was a mistake," Tyler interrupted.

Kate's gaze flew to Tyler's face. His intense expression revealed his determination.

"Just don't say it, Kate." He put a finger under her chin and lifted her face so he could peer into her eyes. "We're not going to rationalize away what happened here. I want you and I'm not ashamed to admit it. But I have a feeling you're not ready for this. This is bigger than simple lust. I'll be over later to talk once I've gotten some shut-eye and can explain properly."

"Tyler, this—we—" Kate began.

He moved his finger to her lips, silencing her. "Later, Kate. We'll talk later. But be warned, we'll probably have to change my job description a little."

Her brow creased as she tried to figure out his meaning. "Your job?"

"That of being your man," he said, eyebrows arched.

Are you my man? Kate stared at him. In one week Tyler had turned her life upside down. His touch had sent her over the edge. He'd made her experience things as never before. It was as if he'd awakened her from a gray world and brought her into one full of color.

"She falls quiet. Probably best for now. Words at moments like this often make awkward situations worse." Tyler pressed his lips to her forehead. "Everything will be fine, I promise. Good night, Kate. Or, in your case, good morning. I'll see you later."

And with that he was gone. Kate locked the door after him, then stared at her kitchen table. She'd let him do unplanned, wonderful things to her. She'd been about to take Tyler into her bedroom and make love with him. She wasn't frigid. She was hot.

But could she just have an affair with him? For she knew that was all it could be. Tyler wasn't the marrying kind. Which wasn't what she wanted, right?

She didn't have time. She had to concentrate on her career. Maybe this *could* be perfect, as Wendy had said. Fulfill her needs without any emotional entanglements that would get in the way of her goals.

Yet, as hot as making love to him would be, the idea of using him for sex sounded cold-blooded. She'd never done anything like that. She realized that was why he'd stopped. Perhaps he knew her better than she knew herself. If they'd made love, she might panic and run away, do something to ruin what was becoming one of the best things in her life. She would doubt him, which would be the worst sin of all.

Chapter Ten

"So I hear from Tara that you're bringing her brother to the company Christmas party this weekend," Marshall said on Wednesday as she placed his pink message slips on his desk. Marshall was still old-fashioned in that he wanted pieces of paper, not e-mails, with names of people he needed to call.

"Yes, he's attending." Kate said. She'd asked him when he came by on Sunday night and he'd agreed. Although they'd watched a movie, he hadn't touched her except to give her one chaste kiss goodbye. She'd been more than a tad disappointed and confused. After all the heat of the morning, the evening had been practically platonic. She hadn't understood or liked the change.

"Good. I'll look forward to seeing him again. And your last finals went well?"

"They did. Classes don't start back up until mid-January. I'm ready for the break."

"I bet you are. I can remember those days. Are you still on target for graduation?"

She nodded. "Yes."

"Well, the senior partners and I are planning to hire three lawyers this spring. As I've told you before, we'd like you to fill one of those spots. You'll need to let us know by the end of January so we can make you a formal offer."

Kate was aware that the big firms often competed for top law-school graduates. "I'm honored. I'll certainly tell you by then," she said.

He studied her a moment. "I hope you choose us. You've been a great paralegal. I'm already going to miss you. So consider tempering my loss by staying on. You have raw legal talent. I'd like to see you hone your skills here. We also have a great program to help our associates study for the bar exam."

She warmed under his compliments. "I will definitely give the firm my full consideration."

Marshall nodded and Kate saw from his body language that she was free to go. As she left the office, she ran into Wendy.

"Hey, are you going to eat with us?" Wendy asked.

"I'm skipping lunch," Kate said. "Marshall's in court tomorrow and I have a few things to finish up. I'm finally taking Frieda to pick up her glasses, so I'm skipping lunch to leave early, instead."

"Oh," Wendy said. "You'll be at the party Saturday, right?"

"Yes, and with Tyler. You can meet him then. He's leaving for Washington, D.C., today, but he's supposed to be back in a day or two."

Wendy smiled. "Didn't I tell you things were going to change? December's been a magical month for you."

"Maybe," Kate said, not that she'd let herself totally believe it. The other shoe usually dropped when she least expected it. She'd learned to be prepared.

"ARE YOU READY?" Tyler inquired as he helped her down from the Hummer. They'd arrived at the country club where the law firm's annual Christmas party was being held.

"As ready as I'll be," Kate said. She put her hand in his, and the ensuing heat fused them. She swallowed. "Are you sure about this?"

"As anything," Tyler said. He opened the heavy wooden door. "Just relax."

"Trying," Kate said as they entered the massive foyer. When she'd met him under his carport, she'd already been wearing her long wool coat. Now she slipped it off and handed it to the coat-check attendant.

"Wow," Tyler breathed.

"What?" She turned to him, wondering if something was wrong.

"You look lovely," he told her. She blushed at his compliment. She wore a fitted sleeveless black sequined dress and black pumps. While definitely conservative in appearance, she was showing more skin than she normally did around her coworkers.

"Thanks. You look great, too."

He did. The event was semiformal, and he'd donned a suit that appeared custom cut for his physique. Kate had a deep sense that she was going to be in trouble tonight—and she would probably enjoy every minute. As he cupped her elbow, longing shot through her. He led her to the ballroom but paused before they entered.

"Mistletoe," he said.

"What?" Kate glanced up to see a strategically placed sprig of greenery. "Oh. That's not really necessary."

He gave her a smile that didn't erase the seriousness in his eyes. "I think tradition should always be observed," he said, and he lowered his mouth for a kiss that, despite its quickness, rattled her and made her lose sense of all time and place. When he broke it off, her lips immediately missed his touch.

"Tyler, Kate! There you two are." Tara approached and Kate wondered how much Tyler's twin had seen. Probably all of it, from Tara's beaming expression. "I've seated both of you at our table. Kate, there are some junior lawyers I want you to meet tonight."

Tyler arched an eyebrow, but Tara simply smiled and told him, "Did you know Marshall offered Kate a job upon graduation?"

"No." Tyler glanced at Kate pointedly.

"Well, he did, and I want to help convince her. So follow me."

Kate had planned to sit with Wendy and her friends. She caught Wendy's gaze and sent her a "Sorry" look. She'd seek her out later and explain the plan had changed. "I guess that's fine," Kate said.

"So, a job offer?" Tyler asked as they followed Tara.

"Yes. I have to decide by the end of January," Kate said.

"A job offer is like money in the bank," Tyler said.

"I know, but I'm not certain that I want to start out in such a large firm."

"It probably has more stability," Tyler observed.

"Yes, but perhaps double the pressure to have billable hours. I just don't know." As Tara began to introduce her to everyone, Kate focused on shaking hands and remembering names.

Dinner was grilled chicken in cream sauce, dessert a strawberry cheesecake, and after the meal, the founding partners made several short speeches and presented a few awards before the dancing got under way. Tyler fit in easily with the group. He was the perfect conversationalist, who could blend humor and reality without sounding pompous or egocentric. He didn't attempt any further physical contact. Still, Kate remained highly aware of him.

"Are you having a good time?" he asked her as the band began its second song.

"Definitely," she said. The junior partners and their spouses were all very nice, and they'd made her feel like one of them and not just Marshall's paralegal. Kate had worried about that "crossing over the other side" predicament.

"Would you like to dance?"

She blinked. Many of the people at their table had escaped to the floor, and Tyler leaned over and took her left hand in his. He toyed with her fingers and Kate gulped.

"Um, I really should talk to Wendy first," she hedged. "Perhaps in a bit?"

"Okay. In the meantime, I'll get you another glass of wine, unless you'd prefer something else," Tyler said.

"Uh, no. Wine's fine." She'd had just one glass with dinner. She detached her hand, stopping the tingle, and made her way over to Wendy.

"I thought you were going to sit with us," Wendy said in greeting.

"Tara put us with her," Kate said. "I'm sorry. I didn't know she had plans for us."

"How are things going?" Wendy asked.

"So far so good," Kate replied. She followed Wendy's gaze to Tyler, who was now talking to Tara. In his hand he held Kate's glass of wine.

"That's his sister, right?" Wendy asked. "I've seen her only a few times."

"Yes," Kate said. She watched for a moment. Tara was gesturing with her hands as she spoke to Tyler. The band had changed songs, and Wendy was suddenly on her feet, Tyler forgotten.

"Hey, I love this song. Let's dance."

Kate glanced at Tyler. He didn't seem too happy with whatever his sister was saying. "Come on," Wendy called, and Kate allowed herself to be dragged out onto the dance floor.

"I CAN'T BELIEVE this. You and Kate are just a joke?" Tara stared at her brother and Tyler averted his gaze so he could watch Kate, who was out on the dance floor without him.

"Tyler," Tara said sharply.

He turned his attention back to his twin. He hadn't planned on revealing anything, but he'd had to say something when she'd told him their mother wanted to meet Kate.

"Not really a joke. We're friends helping each other out. I needed my place cleaned and Kate needed someone to help her get all the meddling matchmakers off her back. So I agreed to play along. That's it. Nothing more. I can't believe you've dragged Mom into this. I can't take Kate to the family dinner tomorrow night. That's going too far."

"Well, you sent her flowers. How was I to know that this was some harebrained scheme? I like her. We did lunch. I want her to join this firm. It would be great for her to date you, and you to settle down. You're despicable, leading Mom and me on."

"I was trying to do things Kate's way."

"What way? Another affair like the ones you always

have? I don't think you know the meaning of *relation-ship*. Tyler, you're thirty-three. Enough is enough. And frankly, anyone can see that Kate's not like that. She may be succumbing to your charms, but she's not like some of the other girls who work here. She has goals, ambitions. Her job is a stepping-stone, not a rest stop."

"I respect that. Who am I to convince her otherwise? I know what I am, sis. I'm a wanderer. I go where the job takes me. I'm away weeks or months at a time. What can I offer Kate?"

"Nothing," Tara said, folding her arms across her chest.

"Exactly. So even if I liked her, uh, that way, what could I do? I don't want Kate hurt, and I certainly don't need Mom getting her hopes up. So let's not make this out into something more than it is."

"It's too late for that," Tara said as she paused and glanced around. No one was paying them any heed. "Maybe it's time you figured some things out."

He frowned. "Like what? My arrangement with Kate is working out great. We like it. We have some chemis-try, but we're both adult enough to know how to handle that. We don't require your meddling."

"Fine," Tara said. "Dinner's at six tomorrow. The whole family is coming. Leo and Ellen will be in New York visiting Ellen's family for the holidays this year, so Mom wanted one meal with everyone present. That includes you."

"I'll be there," Tyler said.

"And Kate?"

"I'll ask her, but don't get your hopes up," he said. Kate was dancing with friends and his gut clenched. She caught him staring and smiled.

"You're in over your head," Tara said, observing the scene.

"Chemistry. That's it. We're two consenting adults. Nothing we can't control," Tyler replied. "I'm the master of the situation. No one will get hurt. We'll just have some fun."

"I'll believe that when I see it. Like I said, Kate's the settling kind, no matter how much you try to fool yourself otherwise. Excuse me. I'm not cutting you off, but I have to talk to that person before he leaves." Tara shook her head and moved off to speak with another lawyer.

Tyler stood there a moment. He could understand Tara's frustration. Deep down he knew Kate was commitment and he wasn't. But he had some intrinsic need to be with her. Although he hadn't been around her long, she seemed to fit him, as if he'd found a part of himself that he hadn't been aware was missing. He wasn't sure what he could offer her besides some mind-blowing passion, but for now, that had to be enough.

So he went out onto the dance floor and claimed his date. "Dance with me?" he asked, wrapping his arms around her as a slower song started.

"Of course," she said, weaving her arms around his neck. Liking the sensation, he moved her closer. "You and your sister appeared to be having an intense conversation."

"Nah. She was just telling me that I'm to be at my parents' house tomorrow night for dinner. I'm supposed to ask you to accompany me. That is, if you want to. You don't have to," he added quickly.

"Do you want me to come?" she asked.

"It might complicate things. My mom's ready for me to settle down."

"Well, perhaps if she thinks I'm dating you the way everyone here thinks you're dating me, she'll leave you alone and lighten up a little. It's the least I can do, since you've helped me out so much."

More bargaining. What he wanted was to kiss Kate again, as he had under the mistletoe. He wanted her to see him as something other than a guy helping her out. "I'd like you to come with me," he said.

"I'd be happy to. Frieda has her glasses and she's back to menacing Orlando's streets, so I'm not needed there. My finals are finished, and all I have left to do is Christmas-shop. After tomorrow, we have only one more weekend before Christmas."

"Yeah, it's on a Tuesday this year." He twirled her and brought her even closer to him.

"The firm shuts down on the twenty-first and won't reopen until January second. I mean, we're open, but very few people are actually at their desks unless there's absolutely something they must do."

"So, a law firm that sleeps," Tyler observed.

"At least once a year, I suppose," Kate said. "Many of the junior partners work long hours, even Saturdays, but that's frowned on during the holidays. I guess the senior partners prefer not to look like Scrooges."

Tyler laughed. "You should tell that to my bosses. Unfortunately, the news never stops. In 2006 I covered the death of former president Ford."

They stepped together in rhythm with the music. "I remember that. He died the day after Christmas."

"I was in Texas on one job, called off that and immediately sent to Washington. I had one detour through New York to photograph New Year's Eve, which turned out to be a quick jaunt. I didn't see my parents until after

Martin Luther King Day. My mother wasn't too happy that I missed Christmas yet again."

"Is that the norm?" She shifted, and he drew her closer still. He liked the way she felt pressed up next to him.

"Most years," he said. "But I've asked for local assignments this season. Stuff within two hours' air travel. I figure they owe me. Still, if the right assignment comes in, I'll be on the next plane. It's what I do."

He pulled her tight one last time before the music changed to something faster and reluctantly he had to let her go. "Shall we get your wine?" he asked.

"Sure. That'd be fine," Kate said. As they left the dance floor, Tara's words rang in his ears. Tyler tried to drown them out, but try as he might, he couldn't. His sister was right. Kate deserved better than a man who would disappear at a moment's notice. He pushed the thought from his head. He'd been honest. He'd told Kate up front about his career demands. But when he walked her to her doorstep following the party, his conflicts again reared their head.

"Would you like to come in for some coffee?" Kate asked.

Coffee. Usually, a euphemism for something else. Tyler sighed. What he wanted and what was the right thing to do were polar opposites. He'd been raised to take the high road. "I'd like to," he said gently, "but not tonight. We've really rushed some things and I'd like to slow down."

"Oh," Kate said.

Okay, that hadn't been spoken correctly. He cupped Kate's face, determined that she not take his refusal the wrong way. "This isn't a rejection. I don't think you know how hard it is for me to say no to you, especially when you're driving me as crazy as you are. I've never wanted anyone as badly as I've wanted you. If I come in, we'll do more than drink coffee."

"Oh," she repeated, eyes wide.

"Oh, yes," Tyler said. "I can't give you commitment. I can only give you passion. So I want you to be sure what you want."

"You," she whispered, and Tyler groaned.

"Yes, but I'm not the settling kind. I'm not Mr. Permanence." He tried again. "Are you sure of what you're getting into?"

"Maybe I don't want anything more," Kate said, her pitch rising. "Maybe I simply want to feel for once in my life. Do you realize you're the only man who's ever called me hot? I want that heat, just want to feel. The rest is unnecessary."

Joyous words for any commitmentphobe, but something held Tyler back. "I'd rather you sleep on it," he said. God knows he needed to. And what did she mean by he was the only man to have ever called her hot? Did she not recognize how desirable she was? Especially tonight? He'd wanted to strip her out of that dress the moment he'd seen it and sink himself inside her.

But he wouldn't. Not until he got a grip on the emotions warring through him like out-of-control wildfires. He gave Kate a kiss on the forehead and drew back. "I'll be by at five to pick you up for dinner. Jeans are fine. Sound okay?"

She nodded and Tyler found he couldn't resist one last taste, so he lowered his lips and kissed her thoroughly. Somehow he managed to get himself back to his house.

Once inside, he watched as Kate flipped lights on and off as she prepared for bed.

Then the reality hit him. Those emotions were so unfamiliar because he'd avoided them all his life. The only commitment he'd ever made was to work. He didn't even promise to attend his family's holiday gatherings. But somehow Kate was special.

With any other woman, he would have accepted her invitation, spent the night and never looked back once he'd left in the morning. But not with Kate. She made him question himself. The thought smacked him that she had the power to claim his heart. She was the woman he could fall in love with.

He sighed in relief. Good thing he'd stopped.

Chapter Eleven

Nora put her binoculars away and sighed. She'd seen the entire kiss, and noted that Tyler had gone home by himself. He'd been a gentleman. Still, Nora didn't trust him. She'd known men like him whose work had been their priority. Her brother, Jake, God rest his soul, had been one of those types. He'd devoted his entire life to the U.S. Navy, leaving behind a string of broken hearts and two marriages. His true passion had been being out at sea, feeling the ocean breeze from the top of an aircraft carrier. When he'd finally retired, he'd immediately become despondent. He'd never quite adjusted to civilian life and, in Nora's opinion, he had died way too young, unlike most of her family, who'd lived far into their nineties.

Nora padded her way back to her bedroom. Kate had fallen for a man with wanderlust, one who, like Jake, could never commit to anything other than his real mistress, work. As she went to bed, Nora still didn't know what to do.

SUNDAY EVENING Kate carefully smoothed out the wrinkle in her chinos. Just ten minutes ago, she'd pressed the pants after taking them out of the dryer. After trying on three different outfits that morning, including jeans, and not being satisfied, she'd tossed the chinos in the wash. She was meeting his family, formally this time, and no matter what Tyler said, she didn't want to appear too casual. So she'd opted for khakis and a cream-colored sweater set. She was simply neutral, which was not at all how she was feeling.

She'd been a bundle of nerves the entire day. Why had she said yes? She'd considered backing out, but changed her mind about that several times, as well. Tyler had attended her party. He'd played his role to perfection. She was the one in way over her head. She'd told him last night she wanted him to sleep with her. Had she come across as desperate? He hadn't seemed to mind her declaration.

At Tyler's knock Kate joined him under the carport. "Hi."

"Hey," he said. He stood there a moment and then leaned over to give her a quick kiss on the cheek. "I hope you're hungry. Mom always serves up a feast."

"Sounds wonderful," Kate said. Fraught, she'd eaten little.

He sensed her unease. "Nervous? Don't be. You already met most everyone."

"True," she said. "But they want to see you, not me."

"Yes, but I want you there," Tyler said.

"They're your family. You don't need me to run interference. I mean, I'm happy to do that. It's only fair turnabout, after all." They were on the highway, and she watched a minivan full of people speed by.

"You're right. I don't need you there. But I want you there. Like I said last night, let's slow this down a little."

"And me going with you to a family dinner will do that?"

Tyler fumbled for words. "Well…uh, yes. I'd like to get to know you, and not just in bed."

"Which I take it you've done a lot," Kate said.

Tyler gripped the steering wheel tighter. "I don't do relationships. All I can say is that I've never been interested in anyone the way I am you."

"Oh."

"Exactly." He watched the road. "I'm intrigued. I enjoy kissing you. But I'm not nine to five. So here I am, in a conundrum unlike any I've ever been in."

"I'm not asking for promises," Kate said. She touched his arm.

He shifted. "No, but as my sister pointed out, you're the type who deserves those promises. You ought to have more than heated sex."

"Why is it that everyone else but me gets to determine what's best for me?"

He exited the freeway. "You shouldn't settle."

"I'm not planning to. I'm not ready to get married. I'm not even out of law school. That's my first priority. Then my job. Then maybe finding someone to spend my life with. As blunt as this is, all I want from you is—"

"Sex," Tyler finished. He paused. "I'm not some stud."

"No, and I'm not saying that. I'm just saying that I'd like to explore the chemistry. I want the heat."

"With me." He turned onto a quiet side street full of mature trees and older homes set on larger lots.

"With you," Kate said. He parked in the driveway and faced her.

"Are you positive of what you're asking?"

"Yes, I am," Kate said.

Tyler pulled her toward him. "I can only give you this."

"That's all I want," she said as his lips descended. She'd longed for his kiss, desired his touch. She lost herself in the moment, until Tyler broke off with a groan.

"We're not in high school. We can't do this here in my parents' driveway."

"We could just go home," she suggested, wild with passion.

"Don't tempt me. Unfortunately, we're expected." He opened his car door, the dinging sound, indicating the keys were still in the ignition, bringing her back to reality.

"We did promise," she said, grabbing her purse.

"Exactly." Tyler hopped down and helped her out. He kissed her once more, then shook himself as if trying to regain control. "Let's go."

Kate lagged a bit behind as Tyler walked through the arched doorway. His voice sounded husky as he greeted his family. "Did you actually set my place?"

"You made it!" From her seat on the couch, a petite brunette who could only be Tyler's mother stood up. "I was starting to have my doubts!"

"I told Tara I'd be here." Tyler strode the rest of the way into the living room, comfortable in a polo shirt and blue jeans. He leaned down to kiss his mother hello. "You know how much I love your ham. Sorry I'm a few minutes late. But I brought Kate to make up for my tardiness."

At his gesture, Kate stepped forward. She clenched her hands behind her back in an attempt to hide her nervousness. Except for small dinners at Nora's or Frieda's, she hadn't really attended large family gatherings.

"Mom, I'd like you to meet my next-door neighbor, Kate Merrill. Kate, this is my mom, Leah. You missed her the day the appliances were installed."

"Nice to meet you," Kate said automatically.

Leah was warm and welcoming. She stood and gave Kate a big hug. "It's wonderful to meet you. Tara tells me you work with her."

"I do."

"Well…" Jamie entered the room, his smile infectious. "Hi, Kate. Tyler hasn't brought a date home since high school."

"Jamie," Tyler warned. His brother just grinned and Kate stepped back as someone asked her what she'd like to drink. A group of kids tore into the room and, upon hearing their grandfather's bellow, took off again.

The dining-room table was huge, and when dinner was served, Kate found herself seated between Tyler and Jamie. Even with ten people around the table, everyone had plenty of space. Not even the children's table at the end, with four wiggling bodies around it, made the dining room seem crowded.

Kate listened, but didn't participate much in the conversation buzzing around her as the Nichols clan discussed everything from politics to New Year's Eve resolutions. Tyler's mother had piled Kate's plate full of ham, sweet potatoes, green beans, salad and two home-made rolls, but Kate had lost her appetite.

"It'll get cold if you don't eat it," Tyler whispered. His breath felt silky in her ear.

Kate jolted, and picked up her fork to avoid replying. She forced herself to take a few bites. She and Sandra had never even had a dining room, much less seven other people plus children to feed. Kate felt awkward, as if she was an interloper. After all, she and Tyler weren't dating. They were only people on a collision course to what would hopefully be great sex.

"So, Kate, we see you've fallen for Tyler's convincing charm," Leo said suddenly, drawing Kate into the conversation. Kate swiveled her head in time to see Leo's wife hit him on the arm with a spoon.

"I, uh—" Kate began.

"He's teasing you," Tyler said. "Everyone knows it was me who fell for you." He put his hand reassuringly over hers. "She's still debating why she should be with me."

"Wise lady to question," Leo said, and ducked the spoon as it headed toward his head.

"Be nice, Leo, or Ellen won't let you out of the doghouse next time," Tyler warned.

"Yeah, you'll be permanently rooming with Sport," Craig shot back.

"The way I see it, Sport did you a favor," Leo insisted.

"Boys," Leah rebuked them quietly, her warning clear. "We have a guest. You've already been vocal enough."

"True." Jamie nodded. "Let's not scare her off. I'm sure Tyler does that well enough on his own."

"Oh, she works with Marshall," Tara said. "She doesn't scare that easily."

"Hey, has anybody heard any new information about the Marlins' new pitcher?" Tyler's father skillfully turned the conversation to sports, and soon his boys were one-upping themselves with their spring-training predictions. As Kate studied Tyler's father, she decided that Tyler would age like his dad.

Chad Nichols had a full head of silvery-gray hair and, except for weathered skin, the same features as his son. Kate shook herself to stop thinking about an older Tyler. She had to be realistic. What they had was lust. As he'd indicated, he couldn't offer more.

Conversation hummed around the table, and Kate concentrated on just listening to the ebb and flow of a large family's chatter. Tyler didn't say much to her during dinner, concentrating on his food as if he hadn't had a home-cooked meal in months. Then again, Kate thought with a wry smile, he probably hadn't. He ate seconds of everything, including the chocolate cake.

Watching him was lethal. His mouth was sensual whether talking or eating, and when he smiled, a twinkle crept into eyes as rich in color as the cake. He took a lot of grief from Jamie, but Kate noticed that he dished it out equally well. The two brothers obviously shared a deep bond. In fact, the whole family did.

"Mom, this was wonderful," Tyler said, pushing his chair back and tossing his cloth napkin onto the table.

"It was good," Jamie agreed. "Although, Tyler, I still like Mom's peach pie better. Kate, you'll have to return when the peaches are ripe and you can eat them right off the trees we have in the backyard. There's nothing like my mom's peach pie."

"That would be nice." Kate gave Jamie a smile. "I like peach pie, especially homemade."

"I'll be sure to bring her by," Tyler said quickly, shooting a warning at Jamie.

"She can come by herself." Jamie raised his eyebrow at Tyler.

"I'm sure she can, but I said I'd bring her."

Tyler's cheek twitched and Jamie laughed at Tyler's response. "Whipped. I never thought I'd see the day." He chuckled some more.

"I can see coming here was a mistake," Tyler said through gritted teeth. "You can't be civil."

"Boys!" Chad's voice boomed over the table.

"Sorry," Tyler mumbled, and Kate wondered if his words were meant for her or his father. Tyler stood. "It's been great, Mom, but it's getting late and we'd best be going. Kate works early tomorrow."

"You do?" Tara asked, surprised.

"Kate?" Tyler prompted. She'd learned to read him, knew he'd reached his patience threshold. She was much the same way. All through dinner an undercurrent had traveled between them.

"Uh, yes. Actually, I do," Kate said as Tyler pulled her chair out so she could leave the table.

"Oh, Tyler, are you sure you and Kate can't stay for a game of cards?" His mother looked so hopeful that Kate experienced a pang of guilt.

"Not tonight, Mom," Tyler said and Kate shivered as she realized the implications. His thigh had been pressed to hers throughout dinner. A tension had tremored between them, demanding to be assuaged. While they were leaving, the night was far from over.

"Well, I'm glad you both were here." Leah stood, resignation evident. She smiled, her laugh lines crinkling as she brightened again. "It's been nice meeting you, dear. Don't be a stranger." Leah picked up a platter and carried it into the kitchen.

"That's our sign we're excused to leave," Tyler said. "Wait here a second."

Tyler went around the table and said his goodbyes. As Kate watched, strange longing overtook her. Each person gave him either a hug or a kiss. Kate tried to remember if that quintessential television family, the Waltons, had kissed and hugged. It was the closest comparison she could find, and it still wasn't close. Not having any family of her own besides Sandra to learn affection from, Kate didn't have the slightest idea what normal was.

"I'll walk you both out." Tyler's father was on his feet, and she noticed he was taller than Tyler. He followed them to the front door. "It meant a great deal to your mother that you came over tonight, Tyler. You are planning on being here for Christmas dinner, aren't you?"

"I'll try. That's all I can promise. You know that, Dad."

"I know." His dad clapped Tyler on the back before they hugged. Then Chad drew Kate into his arms.

The feeling of a father's hug was totally foreign to her. It felt strange, yet wonderfully comfortable. More guilt shot through her. She was deceiving these people, and she felt terrible. She was using Tyler to get the matchmakers off her back. She might have sex with him, but neither of them was serious.

"It was nice meeting you," Kate said, and she found herself relieved as Tyler whisked her away.

They were quiet for the first five minutes of the journey, involved in their own thoughts. Then Tyler spoke up. "So, what do you think of them?"

"I think you're very lucky. I wish I'd had a family like that."

In the darkness Kate couldn't read Tyler's eyes. He

remained quiet for a moment, "Silent Night" playing through the stereo speakers. Finally, he said, "I guess I am, aren't I?"

"Very much," she declared as she let her head sink back against the leather seat.

"I'm sorry about rushing you out of there," he said. "Once my family starts cards, it's an entire evening affair."

"Really, it's fine."

"Good, because what I want to do tonight is make love to you," Tyler said. "That hasn't changed. But, Kate, let me again be honest. I'll be faithful, but work is my focus. If you're really sure you can handle that, then I'm all yours…" He trailed off and let the silence imply the rest. "If not, just tell me to go away and I will leave you alone. I do respect you, Kate, and I only want you to be happy."

His admission shocked her and Kate simply stared straight ahead as he drove into the driveway of his house and shut off the SUV. "I guess we're here." Tyler's words sounded flat as he reached for the car door.

Kate glanced around her, seeing that Nora's house was still lit up like a Christmas tree. She wanted this man. Deep down, could she handle loving him without expecting anything in return? She wasn't the casual type like Wendy, but was it better to have loved once passionately than never to have loved at all? This way at least she'd know heat. She'd know fully she wasn't frigid during lovemaking the way Jack the Jerk had said. She could bury her past, embrace her future with the confidence that she had been well loved—okay, pleasured—once. She'd told him she didn't want commitment. She took a breath, ready with her answer.

"Kate." Tyler's lips were inches from hers.

Kate's breath stilled in her throat. "Yes?"

"At least kiss me once before you decide," he said.

She must have nodded, for immediately his lips found hers. Desire flared as he kissed her gently, and then his mouth became more and more insistent. Fire spread, and her fingers wove into his dark hair. He drew back. "Answer honestly. Do you want to spend the night with me?"

The light from the carport highlighted his face, and Kate could see his taut expression, his features revealing his desire, yet also the fear of her rejection.

"My place or yours?" she asked.

"Come with me," he whispered against her neck.

"I will, as long as you don't stop kissing me."

Tyler's face relaxed, and he gathered her into his arms. "I promise to do that and more, sweetheart. That and more. Come inside."

THERE WERE CANDLES everywhere, Kate thought in wonderment. He'd lit candles while she'd stopped in the bathroom, even putting them just below the windowsills so that the flames reflected off the glass. Suddenly, Kate was in his arms as he carried her.

"My luminary supply. I'll buy more before they have to line the walk," he told her as he laid her on the bed. "I want to see you, see you clearly as I kiss you, as I make love to you. Candles provide the best light. I'm a photographer. I know these things. You are so beautiful."

To stop from babbling, his lips found hers. He tasted of dessert and desire. Finding her own boldness, she darted her tongue inside his mouth to drink in his unique flavor.

She heard him groan. "You're driving me crazy."

He rained kisses down her neck. "I want..." His words drifted away as he ran his hands beneath her sweater. Kate gasped as he touched her breasts.

"So lovely," Tyler murmured as he removed her shirt.

"Tyler!" Kate gasped his name as his kisses and her clothes drifted lower and lower, until the sweater and chinos were somewhere on the floor. His mouth dipped to the juncture of her thighs, and the sensations of his tongue had her fisting her hands in his hair and closing her eyes. She swore she heard sirens blaring as she shattered in sheer bliss.

Lights flashed, Christmas lights, Kate supposed, as caught up in the moment, she reached for Tyler. Her hands under his shirt, she tugged on his belt in an attempt to free him. Within moments he was skin to skin with her.

Could that be her heart pounding so loud?

"Tyler," she moaned. She needed him inside her. Needed to be complete. She pulled him closer, pressed her hands over his ears as she threaded her fingers into his hair.

"I know, darling." He kissed her along her collarbone. She thought she heard him fumbling for something. Protection. He was so sweet and thoughtful. But how was that possible when he was still right next to her and...

"Holy sh—!"

Kate's eyes flew open at the expletive. The voice wasn't Tyler's. Tyler—he was still next to her, buck naked in all his glory.

The harsh, intrusive voice belonged to the fully decked-out firefighter standing in the doorway.

Chapter Twelve

"Kate!"

Kate shuddered as she pushed her chair back from her desk. It was definitely a Monday.

But it had to be better than Sunday—last night. Anything was better than the humiliation of the previous evening. At least here, in the safety of her office cubicle, she could escape the mortification that was now her life on Dogwood Lane.

She'd been so hot last night. So ready. Then the fire of the best lovemaking of her life had literally been doused by the appearance of Orlando's finest. Not that it was their fault. They were just doing their job. Oh, no. The blame lay clearly with Nosy Nora.

The moment had been an awkward one for everyone, including the poor firefighters who'd interrupted the scene. They'd told Kate and Tyler that a neighbor had seen flames flickering and called 911. Both Kate and Tyler had known immediately who that neighbor was. Tyler had never fixed his doorbell, so when no one answered the faint buzz and subsequent knocking, and then the firefighters found the kitchen door unlocked, they did their job and checked out the scene.

Poor guys thought they were saving property and lives. They couldn't have expected to ruin Kate's.

Horrified by the firefighters catching her and Tyler naked, she'd hidden under the sheet until they'd left the bedroom. Then she'd bolted for the bathroom, dressed and slunk home, cursing Nora and her binoculars, which had exaggerated the flames and candlelight.

She'd fled the scene without talking to Tyler, telling him to go away when he came knocking on her door a little while later. She hadn't been ready to face him. She'd seen everything, and boy, was it nice.

No, *nice* wasn't the correct word. *Phenomenal* was closer, but even that didn't do him justice. She'd crossed a line within herself. If she'd been looking for a cosmic sign that she'd made the wrong decision to have sex without commitment, Nora had handed it to her on a platter.

Her phone rang and she answered. "Kate Merrill."

"It's Tyler."

"Hey," she said.

"Are you okay?" he asked.

"Here, I am. I don't know what'll happen when I get home. Everyone on the block was out in your front yard and…"

"The fire truck blocked your escape. No one saw you run across the carport."

"Good try," Kate said, "but everyone saw me."

"It'll be okay, Kate," Tyler consoled.

"Maybe for you. You're never home. You'll be off somewhere. I'll have to go to Nora's Christmas dinner and have people try not to snicker at my being caught in my birthday suit—in your bed!"

"It won't be that bad," Tyler said.

Kate simply held the phone and said nothing. "It'll be that bad?" he asked.

She was exasperated. "I don't know. Maybe I'm making a mountain out of a molehill. But, Tyler, I'm jinxed. Something always goes wrong."

"Listen, Kate, you tell me what it'll take to have a second chance. If I have to book a hotel suite, I'll do it. The fanciest one in Orlando, if necessary, because I'm not having any interruptions next time. I had to take two cold showers. I want you. That hasn't changed. Okay?"

She found herself a little reassured. "Okay."

"Good. Now, when I was at the hardware store this morning, I picked up the stuff to fix your windows. All I'll need is your key and I can go over and install the security locks. Do you want me to swing by your office?"

"There's a spare under that milk can just to the right of my kitchen door. You can use that."

"I'll have everything done before you get home today. And, Kate, don't make any plans for tonight. We're going to finish what we started."

With that, Tyler hung up before she could say anything else.

"Kate?"

Kate jumped as Marshall appeared outside her cubicle. "Yes, Mr. Evans?"

"I've just talked with my wife. We want you to come to dinner at our house this Wednesday night. Are you free?"

She nodded. "Yes."

"Good. Bring that young man of yours, Tara's brother. That way we'll have a foursome for cards."

Kate stared at him and Marshall laughed. "I told

you, I'm not about to allow you to leave this firm. Let the courtship begin. You have the directions, right?"

"Yes." She'd often provided them to Marshall's guests or colleagues.

He smiled. "Then I'll see you Wednesday at six. I'll call Laverne back and tell her it's a date."

"Okay," Kate said as she watched Marshall walk back to his office. Being invited to dinner at a founding partner's house was huge and represented the next step. Then, if she indicated her serious interest in staying, a formal job offer would follow. The company did have some of the best domestic lawyers in the city. She'd learn a lot working with them.

Kate gave herself a little pinch just to make sure that everything was real. Now only her love life was topsy-turvy. Her career was falling into place. At least something was.

AT A LITTLE AFTER THREE, Tyler removed Kate's key from under the milk can. If Nora knew Kate had left a key in such a conspicuous spot, she'd be livid. *Under an object near the door is the first place a burglar looks*, Tyler imagined Nora preaching.

He shook his head and opened the lock. As if he even needed a key to get past this dead bolt. If Nora really wanted Kate's place to be more burglar-proof, Kate should install an alarm system.

Humming, he let himself into the house. Jeckyll wandered in, and with a meow the cat wove himself between Tyler's legs. Tyler found the cat food and filled Jeckyll's bowl. The cat didn't partake. Instead, he stood there as if sizing Tyler up.

"Now, look, cat, after the way you interrupted our

first kiss, you'd best behave. I once had to shoot an attacking tiger with a tranquilizer gun when the guide got injured, so be forewarned. Man to beast, are we clear who's boss?"

Jeckyll just blinked, and Tyler laughed. "I'm talking to a cat. I must be crazy." Jeckyll meowed as if in agreement, sauntered to the food bowl and began eating.

Tyler set his tools on the kitchen table and explored Kate's house. While he'd been inside before, he hadn't been intent on absorbing his surroundings. Curious, he walked through the rooms.

If he wagered a guess, he would assume most of the furniture had belonged to Sandra. There was very little in the house that a twenty-seven-year-old would have purchased, Tyler decided as he fingered one of the yellowing lace doilies that remained on a coffee table.

Given what Kate had told him about her past, Sandra had been the most important person in her life. He could understand why Kate didn't want to part with anything. Plus, with law school, Tyler figured she didn't have the time or the inclination to redecorate. It wouldn't be a top priority for him, either.

Tyler poked his head into the bathroom and grimaced at the sight of pink-and-black tiles. Kate had tried to coordinate the towels, but the permanent fixtures still screamed bad taste, although they had probably been in style when the house was built.

The only room that seemed to say Kate was the master bedroom. Here, she had concentrated her efforts. Around the room she'd scattered frames containing pictures of her as a child. She was in shots with Nora and Frieda, and a woman Tyler assumed was Sandra. A collection of dolls sat on a wall shelf, and an open jewelry box showed off Kate's costume jewelry. The room was soft and romantic, with a floral comforter and matching shams.

Jeckyll hopped up on the bed and plopped in the middle of it. Tyler smiled wryly at the cat's claim. Tyler would certainly like to sleep next to Kate. He'd had every intention of doing just that last night, until he'd become a victim of 911.

He went back into the kitchen and began installing the locks he had purchased earlier that morning at the hardware store. He'd finished all but her bedroom windows, when he heard a knock on the side door. He frowned. Everyone knew Kate wasn't home. Instinctively going into survival mode, Tyler cautiously moved to the window. If a buglar was surveying the house, he'd knock first to make sure no one was home. Tyler pushed the curtain aside. Nora. Figured. He dropped the curtain.

"Hello, Tyler," she called through the glass. "I assumed you were about through, so I'm here to inspect your handiwork. Please let me in."

Tyler checked his anger as he opened the door. "Hello, Nora. Gee, I wonder how you knew I was here."

"I saw you walk over." Nora ignored his sarcasm and immediately tested the kitchen-window locks. "Hmm" was all she said as she went from window to window, Tyler following her by unspoken command.

"I see you haven't finished the bedroom yet," Nora observed. "Saving that for last?"

"I'm not planning on creeping in her windows, Nora," Tyler defended himself. "I just worked out from the kitchen, that's all."

"Yes, I know. I watched you open and close windows as you went."

Boy, she really was a snoop, Tyler thought. Since nothing got by Nora, he'd swear she knew there hadn't been a real fire last night, only candles.

"Well, get these bedroom windows done. I'll wait." Nora settled herself into a chair in the corner of Kate's bedroom. She acted like a woman in charge of Kate's chastity, Tyler thought. She'd deliberately come over to protect Kate's bedroom, to make sure he'd get no ideas, especially after last night. To keep from saying something he'd regret, Tyler concentrated on installing the window guards.

"You know you'll break her heart," Nora said, ending the silence a few minutes later.

"What?" Tyler turned from where he was finishing the last lock and looked at Nora.

She eyed him, her gaze unflinching. "I said you'd break her heart. I argued with Frieda about it yesterday before she left for Colorado, but as usual, she didn't listen. So I decided to take matters into my own hands. You'll only hurt Kate and I won't allow it."

Flabbergasted by the full-frontal attack, Tyler could only stare.

Nora nodded, as if his silence confirmed her statement. "You're not the type of man to settle down, Tyler Nichols. Kate should have someone stable in her life, like my Niles."

"Your Niles is probably a nerd." Tyler winced. That had sounded harsh and bitter. But he'd simply reacted and lashed out.

Nora didn't appear in the least perturbed by Tyler's statement. "Niles might be a bit nerdy, but he's very stable. He wants the simple life. A wife. Kids. A home. He may not be as good-looking as you, but at least he's not constantly off jet-setting around the world."

"I don't jet-set," Tyler managed to say, caught unprepared by Nora's offense. "I report. There's a difference. A big one."

"No, there's not," Nora stated matter-of-factly. "Don't even defend yourself by telling me you sleep in a tent versus a hotel. It doesn't matter. It still means you're gone and that you won't be here when Kate needs you."

She blinked once behind the cat-eye frames and Tyler wondered if she'd ever been a teacher. Her gaze reminded him of Mrs. Burgoyne right before she'd given him a detention his senior year of high school.

"Kate is precious. She's been like a daughter to me. She hasn't had it easy. Her mother was always leaving her, until finally Sandra put her foot down. So have you no conscience? You'll only be doing the same thing."

"Kate and I have an understanding," Tyler said. While true, somehow saying it to Nora made the statement sound incredibly lame.

Nora suddenly attacked Tyler from another flank. "She deserves more than a quick roll in the hay. The way you tried to seduce her last night was not neighborly, Tyler. It was indecent."

Indecent, hell. It had been the most fantastic lovemaking of his life, until Nora had interfered. "Well, you certainly fixed it, didn't you?"

Nora didn't look at all sorry. "Yes, I did, and I have no regrets. Do yourself a favor and forget Kate. I know this all started out as some scheme to get matchmakers off her back. Fine, I'll lay off with Niles. But only if you step away and leave her alone."

Nora inspected the last two windows before waving a finger under his nose. "You'll introduce her to a world she can't have, Tyler Nichols. The only stable person Kate ever had in her life was Sandra. Kate doesn't know how to handle smooth-talking men like you, men who promise what they'll never deliver. You'll break her heart. Mark my words. Find yourself another girl to toy with. I'm sure you have a black-book full."

Even in the worst battle scenes, Tyler had never lost control, and he wasn't going to start now. So he simply remained silent and gathered up his tools. Nora reminded him of his own grandmother. Once set on her ways, there was no deviation. She was stubborn to a fault. He knew it was useless to argue.

His cell phone began trilling, meaning he had a call. Ignoring Nora's raised eyebrows, he answered. "Tyler Nichols."

"Ty!"

Tyler turned his back on Nora's scowl. She already believed the worst of him, so why bother changing the way he talked to his assignment editor? Especially after last night. "Hey, Jess, baby. What's up now?"

"Tornado, and you're covering the damage."

"Tornado?" Tyler repeated. "It's drizzling outside, Jess, but that's it."

"No, not here." Jess named a town about an hour away. "You're closest. Get there."

"I thought tornadoes don't happen in December."

"They're rare, but not impossible," Jess said. "Remember the one that touched down in Daytona around Christmas? The damage was extensive in Tallahassee and Jacksonville. Even worse were the storms that went through in February that killed nineteen."

Tyler hadn't been in the United States at the time, but he'd heard about those. Many people had spent the day after Christmas cleaning up, and Florida had suffered another blow a few months later. "This state is becoming tornado alley," he said.

"Anyway, we're sending you down there as soon as you get to the airport. We've got the Cessna standing by."

"On my way, Jess. You know I come when you call." He hit the end key on his phone. "My assignment editor," Tyler added for Nora's benefit.

"You're leaving." Nora's tone reflected her disapproval.

"It's my job. You'll hear about the tornadoes on the news." Tyler walked into the kitchen, grabbed his tools and pocketed Kate's key. "Tell Kate her windows are done and I'll call her tonight."

"You're going to break her heart," Nora repeated.

"She'll understand. This is my job." *Nosy, know-it-all neighbor.* Tyler slammed the door for emphasis as he left.

WHEN KATE ARRIVED HOME later that night, the first thing she noticed was that Tyler's house was dark and his SUV was gone. Not a good sign. Not when she needed to talk to him.

Kate filled Jeckyll's empty food bowl before opening the refrigerator. She hadn't shopped lately. She debated calling for pizza, then decided against it. She'd just make herself a little rice and some frozen peas. Not very exciting, but they would be enough to curb her hunger since she'd had a big lunch. Her home phone rang when she was in the middle of measuring water into the rice cooker.

"Hello?"

"Hi," Tyler said. Kate glanced out the window. His house was still dark.

"Hi back. Where are you?"

"Stop looking out the window. I'm not there." Kate let the curtains flutter closed as he named the town he was in.

"Are you there?" Tyler asked when she didn't say anything.

"I'm here," Kate answered. She reached for a bowl.

"Good. I thought I'd lost cell signal or something. Just wanted to tell you I finished your windows, and ask you to watch my house for me until I get back. I'm not sure how long that will be—it depends on when the governor arrives, which will be either tomorrow afternoon or Wednesday morning."

"Governor?" Kate said.

"Yeah, he's coming to assess the storm damage."

"Tyler, what are you talking about?"

"I forgot." He sounded perturbed. "Turn on the TV. That storm that just gave us drizzle nailed other parts of Florida. A tornado even hit a school and the gym roof blew off. Luckily, no one was injured."

Kate felt a sick to her stomach. "I'll have to watch tonight."

"Do. I'm here until the governor shows, then I'll be on my way home. I'm sorry I had to drop everything and go, but I'll see you the moment I get back. Call me if you need me for anything."

"Okay," Kate replied, a tad miffed. She needed a dinner date on Wednesday, and he wasn't going to be around. She sighed. Hadn't he told her that he couldn't be more than he was? Why had she pretended otherwise?

From the tone of his voice she could tell he was a man in his element. This was the news drama Tyler loved. How could she compete with that? "I'll make sure everything is okay with your house," she said.

"Great. I'll see you soon. Sorry I'm not there. I was looking forward to tonight."

Sure he was. He'd wanted sex. So had she. But as he'd always indicated, his work was his mistress. And she'd come calling.

Kate heard him say, "What? Another one?" and realized he wasn't talking to her. "I've got go, Kate. They've just found some people in an overturned mobile home. They're alive, and rescue workers are getting them out now."

With that, the phone in Kate's hand went dead. Tyler hadn't even bothered to say goodbye.

Kate slowly hung up and went back to making her pathetic excuse for a dinner, exhaling the frustration she felt despite her sympathy for the tornado victims. What had she been thinking, depending on him in the first place? He'd made her no promises. He'd told her how things would be. Kate squeezed back a tear. He should have been here for her! No. She angrily pushed that thought aside. She had no claim on him. It was her fault for having unrealistic expectations and falling for a wanderer who would never settle down. He could make love to her, but he couldn't give more than that.

Kate raised her chin. She'd either have to cancel Wednesday or go alone. Besides, being single was something she was used to.

THE NEXT AFTERNOON Kate jumped as her phone buzzed and Marshall's voice came over the intercom. "Kate? Will you join me in my office, please?"

"Yes, sir. I'm on my way." Kate released the talk button and brushed some lint off her blue linen skirt. The doors to Marshall's office were open and Kate rapped on the wooden frame. Entering, Kate was surprised to find a few other people were in the room.

"Kate." Marshall strode over to her. "Thanks for joining us. I wanted to introduce you to some of the senior partners. This is Kate Merrill, whom I've been telling you about."

Kate froze a smile in place and somehow managed to hold her own as the partners asked her questions. From the expression on Marshall's face, she knew her performance had pleased him. He was taking his wooing of her into the firm seriously. He even announced that he'd contacted several of her professors.

"Anyway," Marshall was saying, "my wife decided that an intimate party for four wouldn't be enough. Now that we're empty nesters, Laverne's determined to liven the place up as much as possible, especially during the holidays. Therefore she's planning to have a houseful of people to entice Kate to the firm."

Kate wanted to sink through the floor. A houseful? She hadn't even had the chance to tell Marshall, who'd been in court all morning, that Tyler wasn't in town.

"You're quite serious about your young man, right, Kate?" Marshall beamed at Kate.

"Um, uh…" She stalled, trying to figure out the diplomatic approach. "But we're both career people and he's on assignment, covering the tornado, and—"

"He's Tara McCabe's brother," Marshall interrupted. The senior partners nodded.

Kate tried again. "Yes, but he's on—"

Marshall was bulldozing ahead. "We're going to hold a brief meeting now, but I wanted you to meet everyone before we started. Thanks, Kate."

"Yes, thank you." Kate gritted her teeth and left the room. Great. Tyler wasn't her boyfriend and she certainly wasn't serious about him. Boyfriends were around. Instead, she was chasing a man who was somewhere over the rainbow, shooting the aftermath of a tornado.

In the end, she could depend only on herself. Yes, she'd go alone, and damn the consequences.

EARLY WEDNESDAY MORNING, Tyler felt his cell phone vibrate. Even if he could answer it, now was not a good time to talk, anyway. He was in a helicopter with the governor, documenting the tornado's devastation and the governor's reaction to it. There would be no doubt; two counties would be declared disaster areas.

Irritated with the buzz, Tyler decided to at least find out who was calling. He grimaced when he read the name on the display. His sister. It figured. She was probably annoyed that he'd taken Kate to the family dinner and then immediately gone out of town on assignment. Well, he didn't have time to deal with Tara at this second. If she really needed him, she could text. Within a few minutes, his phone vibrated again, indicating she'd done just that. Tyler opened the phone, pressed a few buttons and found himself extremely angry as he began to read his sister's message about Marshall's party.

Chapter Thirteen

For the fourth time Kate made a wrong turn, but finally she'd found the gatehouse to the exclusive community Marshall and Laverne lived in. The guard waved her through, and Kate drove past huge houses on three-acre lots. Kate squared her chin. She could do this, even if it meant doing it alone.

"Kate!" Laverne opened the door herself. She ushered Kate in and took the wrap from her shoulders. "Tyler's not home yet?"

"He's detained with work. He's on assignment covering the tornado damage."

"Oh, yes. It's all over the news. So terrible, and right before the holidays. I can't even begin to imagine," Laverne said.

"You have a lovely home," Kate said.

"Thank you."

Although *lovely* didn't describe it, Kate thought, sizing up the expensive marble tile covering the floor of the large foyer. Everything was decorated for the holidays, so that the house resembled a featured house in an upscale designer-home magazine.

"We couldn't have any kids ourselves, so we adopted

six foster children over the years. They filled every inch of this space," Laverne said as she took Kate's coat.

From her many encounters with Laverne, Kate knew the older woman was friendly and generous.

"Marshall and I rattle around this place, but we're not ready to downsize. Once everyone arrives for Christmas, this place will be crowded. I'm a grandmother several times over already, and one more's on the way. Everyone's in the library. By the way, great dress, Kate. Black's your color."

Glad she had worn a festive bolero jacket with her plain linen black sheath, Kate followed Laverne into the library. She accepted the glass of white wine Laverne offered her.

"Let me introduce you around," Laverne said. "Marshall had a last-minute phone call and will join us in a moment."

"Kate, glad you made it," one of the partners she'd met earlier that day said. By the time dinner was announced, Kate found herself enjoying the evening.

"I always keep a catering firm on call," Laverne confided as she took Kate's arm and led her in to dinner. "I can't cook, and with six kids, I needed the help. Now, you're seated here, next to Marshall." Kate noticed the seat to her right remained open.

Conversation buzzed around the long formal table. Kate had finished her fruit plate, soup and salad, and was waiting for the main course, when Marshall stopped debating politics with the female judge to his left and turned to Kate.

"So, Kate, have you heard from that young man of yours?"

Kate's eyes widened. "Not today. I try not to bother

him when he's working. He's covering the tornadoes. As you know, he's a photojournalist."

"A man should never be a slave to his job. His family should always be first," Marshall declared, touching his wife's hand.

Kate averted her head. Love like Laverne and Marshall's was rare, and something Kate doubted she'd ever find. The flaky salmon had lost its flavor in Kate's mouth.

Somewhere in the other room a doorbell chimed.

Marshall nodded, satisfied. "Ah. Hopefully, our last guests."

"Excuse me." Laverne rose and left the table.

"Look who I found, everyone." Laverne returned with Tara McCabe. As Tara walked into the room, Kate's hands shook. She clenched them under the table and attempted to calm herself.

"Miss me, darling?"

Kate almost jumped out of her seat as the husky voice breathed down on the back of her neck. As she whirled to face Tyler, her hand flailed and caught the water goblet.

The crystal didn't break when it hit the table, but the liquid seeped over the red damask tablecloth, making the area between her and Marshall's place settings soppy.

"Tyler!" Shock had Kate struggling for composure.

"In the flesh, darling." While no one else could, Kate sensed his anger. "I'm sorry I'm late."

With that, Tyler hauled her to her feet and kissed her. She felt her left foot lift off the ground, as if she were an actress in a classic movie. Tyler kissed her just long enough for the kiss to be socially acceptable, then he released her. He sheepishly faced their audience. "Sorry. I've missed Kate while I've been gone."

Overpowered by the kiss, Kate stood as if rooted. Marshall got up and shook Tyler's hand. "It's good to see you again, Tyler. I was worried you wouldn't make it at all."

"It was touch-and-go for a while, but of course I wouldn't miss being here."

Conversation returned to normal levels as Tyler took the empty seat to Kate's right. He ran a forefinger lazily over Kate's neck. She quivered from the sensation he sent shimmering down her back. When he leaned over, Kate immediately felt heat spread through her. "Are you really full, or did you just lose your appetite at my appearance for a dinner you forgot to tell me I was supposed to attend?"

"Why should I have bothered?" she asked so that only he could hear. "That would have been presumptuous. Your job comes first. You made that clear. I'm not trying to trap you. You wouldn't have been in town. Now, eat your salmon. People are staring."

"That's only because you're so lovely. I like that dress."

"Flattery won't get you out of this one, Tyler." Kate reached for her wine goblet and took a sip.

"Funny, I didn't think I was the one attempting to get out of something."

Kate faced Tyler. He forked another bite of food into his mouth and raised both eyebrows at her.

"I had everything under control. I'm used to doing things alone. You didn't have to show up," she whispered.

"Yes, I did." Tyler's lips were almost on hers. "I heard

from my sister that you were supposed to be taking me to a party, one that you failed to tell me about."

"It was easier that way."

"You and I have a lot of unfinished business, Kate."

He meant lovemaking. The thought of finally consummating her passion with Tyler thrilled and terrified her at the same time.

"Break it up, you two lovebirds," Laverne called from her seat. "Dessert's about to be served, and if you two don't quit making eyes at each other, Tyler will never finish the main course."

"That's all right, Laverne. I'm savoring my dessert right now."

"Tyler!" Kate's face flamed with embarrassment. Laverne laughed, obviously thinking the situation romantic and delightful.

Kate managed to make it through the rest of the evening, despite the tension just below the surface of any interaction between her and Tyler. After a few parlor games like Pictionary, the night wound down, and Kate and Tyler made their way to leave.

"That went pretty well, I think," Tyler said as he followed Kate to her car.

"Didn't you drive?"

"I had Tara pick me up at my house. You're my ride home. Please."

"Get in," Kate said, not wanting to leave him stranded at her boss's house. She started the car, and soon they were en route. She leaned forward and touched the volume knob on the radio. "I love this song. Do you mind?"

"No," Tyler replied as instrumental Christmas music began to play.

Grateful for the diversion, Kate turned up the volume

so that holding a conversation was almost impossible. She shifted slightly to study his profile. Once again she had to acknowledge that he was a gorgeous man. Dark hair, almost black, framed his face. His nose fit him, and an age-old break added character and intrigue. As attractive as ever, and still out of her league.

"You've grown quiet," he said, reaching over to turn down the volume.

"I was listening to that song."

"It was a commercial. The song ended a few minutes ago." Tyler gave her a small smile.

"Oh." Kate clamped her mouth shut.

"Honesty, Kate." He ran two fingers down her cheek. "We may be lying to the world about our relationship, but with me you must be honest. That's all I ask. I shouldn't have heard from my sister that you needed me to attend that dinner with you."

The car grew quiet except for the radio host's voice announcing the next selection. "I shouldn't be holding you back," she said. "You were working. I could handle the dinner myself."

"You didn't have to. If I know what's going on, I can come through for you."

"But we said no expectations. No commitments."

"Kate, that's only about marriage. We're friends. I want you. Do you think I just want to crawl into bed with you and that's it? That would make me petty and a cad."

Kate stayed silent. "You've had a run of bad people destroying your self-esteem, haven't you? Whoever he was, he was a jerk."

"How did you know it was a guy?"

"It always is."

A lump formed in her throat. They were safely underneath her carport and she shut the engine off. "I was fine attending alone. You were with the governor. I'm just sorry you got dragged into something else. We keep digging ourselves in deeper and deeper."

Tyler leaned over the center console until his nose almost touched hers. "Stop apologizing. I don't do anything I don't want to do. Never have, never will."

Unlike her, he probably hadn't. His lips were close, and she focused on his mouth as he bestowed a kiss that made her toes tingle. She closed her eyes, letting his magic sweep her away.

In a heartbeat, she realized several things. First, she desired him more than any other man. But second—and more important—she'd fallen for him.

He was the man she'd been looking for, the one who could be her hero, the one who could stand behind her.

The enormity of the truth hit her. How could she so deeply love someone who wasn't marriage-minded? Eventually, she wanted that. She didn't want to love someone who would abandon her. She'd had enough of people like her mother and Jack doing that. If their actions had hurt, how much more painful would losing Tyler be?

She ended the kiss and drew away quickly, throwing Tyler off balance. He slipped forward on the seat.

"Sorry," Kate said as he caught himself. Before he could recover, she opened the door and jumped out of the car.

She was fumbling for her house key, when Tyler took it from her fingers. "Stop running, Kate. Face whatever it is you're fleeing from this time."

"You want honesty, Tyler?" she snapped, angrier with

herself and her newly discovered emotions, feelings that would never be returned. "The truth is that I'm afraid. I want you, too, and—and damn the consequences!"

"Thank God," was all Tyler said. He opened the door to the house, scooped Kate up and carried her over the threshold. She heard the door close, but still he didn't set her down. Then she heard Jeckyll meow, but ignored him, too, as Tyler carried her to the bedroom and kicked the door shut.

Her eyes widened as he lowered her gently to the bed. "Let me tell you some truths, Kate Merrill. You are a beautiful, intelligent woman. Your kisses are full of passion, and you drive me absolutely crazy. You dominate my thoughts."

Kate lay on the bed, looking up at him. The only illumination in the room came from the glow of Christmas lights slanting through the blinds. Tyler's face was in shadow, making him dark, handsome, mysterious and incredibly sexy.

He stood over her, a classic position of dominance, but Kate wasn't afraid. She was excited, alive with the sensations he stirred in her. This was a man who would take her to the heights she'd dreamed of but had never experienced. She reached up and dragged him down onto the bed.

Tyler succumbed, his hands cupping her face. He brought his lips to hers. The kiss was sweet yet needy, and he plundered her mouth.

He took his time making love to her, escalating the urgency between them as he caressed every part of her body. Kate grew daring, as well, holding him in her hand until he pulled away, unable to take more. "You're so hot," he murmured against her neck as he kissed her mouth.

"Really?" The word slipped out, as for one brief moment reality entered and she had to know, had to be certain.

"Absolutely hot. But you're doubting me. Why?" Tyler asked. He balanced on one forearm, his fingertips tracing patterns on her cheek.

"I was told I was frigid," Kate admitted.

Tyler slid his hand between her thighs. "Not with me," he said, and she could see the truth in his eyes as he gave her another long kiss.

Then Tyler was over her and in her, and Kate's body stretched with the welcome intrusion as he began to stroke, his movements having her clutching the sheets as her own release began. "See how hot and slick you are?" he told her, using even more words to encourage her to let go, until Kate threw her head back and screamed until Tyler completed her.

He made love to her several more times throughout the night. After each lovemaking he held her tight and they talked. She told him about Jack, she told him more about her childhood and she told him her concerns about Marshall's job offer.

"If it's too good to be true," she said.

"Not all things fit that cliché," Tyler said as he held her tight.

"I have been considering it. Marshall said the firm has a program to help me study for the bar exam. I wouldn't get that type of support in a smaller firm. I know everyone, and I like the company. It's an ethical, sound place."

"If you change your mind, you can always find a new job down the road. People do that all the time."

"True," Kate said. She snuggled closer. It was almost morning. "I'll be struggling to stay awake today."

"I guess that's a bad thing," Tyler said, running his fingers over her thighs. A part of him stirred as he was ready for her again.

"You're insatiable," she said as he pulled her on top of him.

"Yep. I can't get enough of you. Sleep's overrated." And as he kissed her, Kate gladly succumbed.

Tyler was still there when her alarm went off for the third time, signaling that she had to stop hitting the snooze button and get up. Kate stepped out of bed and escaped into the bathroom. He used her hall bath and she found him dressed and sitting at her table when she made her way into the kitchen.

"Good morning," he said. "I took the liberty of making you some coffee."

"Oh, you are a god," Kate said, accepting the cup of black brew Tyler held out. She added a teaspoon of sugar. "I'll need all the caffeine I can get today."

"I'm going to be a cad and go home and back to sleep. Haven't received my new assignment yet, but I'm sure Jess will be calling soon."

"Jess?"

"My assignment editor. Technically, I'm out of the Orlando bureau because I live here, but I go wherever I'm sent. I've worked my way up to having my choice of some plum assignments."

"You're one of the best," she said.

"I guess, although I wasn't part of the group of company photographers who won the Pulitzer. I have to admit to some professional jealousy. I want one of those someday."

Kate shook her head. "I go for safe and secure and you go for danger."

"You were pretty dangerous last night," Tyler said. "I have marks on my back to prove it."

Kate set her coffee down. "Sorry about that."

He stood next to her, invading her space. "Don't be. When you're with me I want you to lose yourself. If you want it, ask. That's all you have to do."

The intensity in his eyes scared her somewhat. If she asked, would he love her back? Could he prioritize her over his jet-setting job?

"Like last night," Tyler continued. "All you had to do was tell me there was a dinner you needed me to be at. I have some negotiability with my schedule. I would have been there for you."

"I didn't want to intrude on your work," Kate said.

"Let me make that choice. Tell me next time you need something."

"I'll remember," Kate said.

"Good." Tyler seemed satisfied. "Now, I'm going to try and sneak out of here without Nosy Nora seeing."

"Ha. I wish. She'll be grilling me later, I'm sure," Kate said.

"Then say we're very happy," Tyler said. He leaned down and gave Kate a long kiss before heading home.

Kate finished her coffee and gathered her thoughts. She fed Jeckyll and glanced at the wall calendar. Today and tomorrow were it—her last two workdays before Christmas and New Year's.

She made her way to the door and opened it.

"Nora!" Kate almost dropped her purse. "You scared me."

"That's why you should look first," Nora chided, but not as sharply as normal. She appeared distracted. "I could use a favor. Only Niles was supposed to arrive this weekend, but now Patti and Cindy are staying here, too."

The names sounded familiar. "Who?" Kate asked, focusing on the fact that Nora hadn't mentioned Tyler.

"Patti is my late husband's sister. Cindy is her sister-in-law. I'm already going to have Dora—that's my sister—and Niles at my place for the holiday. I'm out of room, and Frieda's house is locked up tight and I don't have a key. Besides, I don't want to put them there."

"Didn't Sandra have them stay over here once?" Kate remembered.

"She did a few times before you moved in, and once after, when you were seven. So can I impose?" Nora asked. "It's only until the twenty-sixth. They swear they're leaving then. And they won't even arrive until Sunday."

"Uh, sure," Kate said, wondering how Tyler would take to two elderly chaperones staying in Kate's house for three nights. Then again, Kate could see Tyler at his house.

"You're a lifesaver, Kate. I'll talk to you when you get home. I don't want you to be late for work," Nora said. With that, she tightened her housecoat and headed back across the street.

Kate beat Marshall to the office by a good half hour. "It was a great time last night," he said as he sorted through the paperwork on his desk. "Everyone was very impressed with you."

"Thank you," Kate said. She stood there for a moment until Marshall glanced up.

"Yes, Kate? Something else?"

"I've decided that I'd like to pursue employment discussions with you," she said.

Marshall's face split into a wide smile. "Excellent. That's news I like to hear. I'll call Human Resources and have them draft a formal offer. You'll have it by the middle of January, and we can negotiate if necessary."

"Thank you," Kate said.

"No, thank *you,* Kate. You've been a great paralegal. You're sharp and tenacious. You'll be a fantastic lawyer."

Kate had a skip to her step as she left his office. When Wendy arrived for lunch, she only added to Kate's enthusiasm.

"Kate! It's all over the building. Congratulations!" Wendy stood outside Kate's cubicle. "I'm glad. I didn't want you to leave."

"Well, it depends on the offer. Until then, nothing's final."

"Oh, it'll be a good one. I can't tell you how happy I am that you succeeded. Just don't forget your paralegal friends when you cross over to the other side and become one of the suits."

"I won't," Kate promised.

"Oh, I know you won't." Wendy pushed a strand of brown hair out her face. "You aren't the type to turn your back on anyone, especially your friends. So, what do you think Tyler will say about all this? You'll have to make sure he takes you out somewhere great for a celebratory dinner. Or, I could call my cousin. Edwin would be willing to splurge big bucks on you. He's always had the biggest crush on you, and it's not like you and Tyler are engaged or anything."

"No," Kate agreed. "But he's in town and things are progressing nicely."

Wendy glanced at her watch. "Tell me at the restaurant. We're wasting precious minutes."

"Okay." Kate grabbed her coat, set her phone to voice mail and followed Wendy out to the busy Chinese place around the corner.

"So you and Tyler are getting along?" Wendy asked as she and Kate took seats in a corner booth.

Kate colored. "Yes."

Wendy tilted her head. "There's more."

Kate nodded. "I'm not…" How to say it, even to her best friend? "He thinks I'm hot."

Wendy leaned forward, put her hand up and gave Kate a high five. Kate slapped Wendy's hand, and then they moved so that their heads were closer.

"I knew it wasn't you," Wendy said. "Jack was a bastard. I'm so happy for you."

"Tyler's great. It was phenomenal…" Kate filled her friend in, of course skipping some juicy details.

"So you didn't make love that night I came over?" Wendy asked suddenly, as if realizing she'd been had.

"No."

Wendy snorted. "I don't believe it. Really? You had me so fooled."

"Well, that was the plan. I know this sounds terrible, but I guess I led you on. You and the girls were always trying to fix me up, and well, I figured that if I pretended Tyler was my boyfriend, you'd all back off without me having to say it."

"You could have just said it," Wendy said. She didn't appear pleased.

"I know. I'd intended on going to the party. But Tyler did just move in that night and we met when he borrowed my cleaning supplies. So I volunteered to help. And Nora showed up with a stew and—"

Wendy made a stop motion with her hand. "I get the picture. Whenever Nora's involved, the situation evolves into a life of its own."

"Exactly. I lost track of time, and then you arrived and—"

"I jumped to the wrong conclusions," Wendy said with a shake of her head. "But what about the flowers?"

"I guess Tyler didn't like my plan, either. He was really interested. Is interested," Kate corrected. "I even had dinner with him and his family last Sunday."

"Wow! He's taken you to meet his family already. He sounds like a great guy."

"He is," Kate admitted.

"I hear a *but* coming," Wendy said.

"He's great. Charming. Everything I want in a man."

"But..." Wendy prodded.

"His job. One minute he's here and the next he's off somewhere else. He's climbed Everest, Wendy. He's traveled with marine units in Iraq. He said he'd be there for me..."

"But you're afraid he won't. You're afraid he might be like your mom."

"He's not the settling kind. The next cool assignment, the next photography challenge, and Tyler will be on the road for what could be months. He's a nomad. How can you tame the wind?"

"You've fallen in love with him, haven't you?"

Kate averted her head and studied the waitress serving the next table. "Yes."

"Have you told him any of this? Have you talked to him?"

"He told me I could ask him anything," she said. "But guys always say that. As it is, I've got to tell him I have Nora's out-of-town company staying with me."

Kate explained and Wendy made a face. "I'm nominating you for sainthood," her friend said.

"It's fine."

"Just move in with Tyler," Wendy suggested.

"We're certainly not to that point," Kate said. She wasn't normally the type to wallow, and while she trusted Tyler, she didn't trust his work. The world had been quiet—for the time being.

That night, however, found Tyler still at home. He called her the moment she got in. "I'm cooking," he said without preamble.

"You cook?"

"Not well, but I'm trying to impress you. I can make spaghetti and anyone can heat up garlic bread." Kate spotted him standing in his kitchen window. He waved at her.

"So is this an invitation?" she teased.

"Yes. I've missed you," he said.

"Give me a few minutes," Kate said. She changed out of her work clothes, glanced at her mail, decided there wasn't anything that couldn't wait and walked next door.

As soon as she entered, Tyler lowered his lips to hers. The kiss was gentle, and he explored her mouth tenderly, as if she were fragile glass.

"Wow," she said.

"Welcome home," he said. "The food's ready, so let's eat."

"Okay." She sat at the kitchen table and Tyler poured her a glass of red wine.

"How was your day?" he inquired. She laughed and he frowned. "What?"

"This is funny. You. Me. It's domestic."

His expression didn't change. "And there's something wrong with that?"

She shook her head. "No."

"Would you rather me greet you at the door and tell you that I've been waiting all day to take your clothes off?"

His words emboldened her. He'd told her all she had to do is ask. She got up and stepped forward, invading his space. "So, is undressing me what you really want? Because I'm thinking that I'm not all that hungry right now."

"Really?" he asked, eyes darkening. "I am."

"I see," Kate said, lacing her arms around his neck. She brought her lips close. "Then let's eat."

They ate the food much later and, garlic flavoring mingling on their breaths, tumbled back into bed after dessert.

This time he let her lead. He was so strong, yet so tender. She'd never felt freer, more in control, or more in love. She'd been made for this, made for him, she thought as she ran her fingers over his smooth chest.

"Kate." He groaned out her name.

"It's okay, Tyler," she whispered as he took over. "I want you just as much."

Skin warmed skin, and his hands cupped her breasts.

His mouth suckled and laved, and as his lips moved over her flesh, Kate lost control.

Her limbs loosened, tightened with the sensations he sent through her, and as his lips returned to recapture hers, Kate grew even bolder.

She touched and tasted him. When he entered her, she was ready. She stilled for a moment, reveling in the intimacy. Then his hips began to undulate, thrusting slowly at first, then faster, harder, until Kate was right there on the amazing journey with him. She peaked first, then with him, and then again as he went over the edge.

He held her tightly afterward, her head snuggled against his firm chest. She relaxed, and wasn't sure how long she slept before she found herself waking up, looking into his eyes and starting all over again.

So this is what love is all about, Kate thought, feeling Tyler stroking her hair. Last night hadn't been a fluke. She'd been well loved two nights in a row. She felt so complete. Healed from her demons.

"You're quiet," Tyler whispered, his breath warm on her cheek.

"I was just thinking," she replied as she began to drift off. The mattress dipped as Tyler raised himself up on an elbow. He traced her cheek with the back of his forefinger.

"Penny for those thoughts," he said. "Share them with me, sleepyhead."

The moon had set, and the room had drifted into darkness, except for an occasional twinkle from a Christmas light outdoors. Kate closed her heavy eyelids, and she could feel him caressing her cheek.

Was he still waiting for her answer? She couldn't tell

him the truth. Not yet. Not when she knew he didn't love her back. "You were phenomenal," she murmured, and then sleep swept her away.

TYLER STARED DOWN at her face, angelic in slumber. He'd wake her up in plenty of time for her to return to her house and get ready for work.

He sighed, rolled onto his back and studied the ceiling. Tumultuous thoughts jumbled his brain as he struggled to sort out his feelings. Their lovemaking was without a doubt the best he'd ever had. He was connected to Kate in a way that he'd never been attached to anyone else.

Nora's words haunted him. She'd predicted Tyler would hurt Kate. That was the last thing he wanted. He cared for her a great deal— No, he loved her, he realized. She'd become extremely important to him, almost as important as his work and the accolades he craved. But would his feelings be enough? Could he make something work between them with a job as demanding as his?

He resolved to try, and prayed he wouldn't somehow mess everything up in the process. He leaned over her. She was as beautiful as an angel. He kissed her forehead once, the kiss featherlight. "I love you, Kate. It'll work out. I promise."

Chapter Fourteen

The insistent ringing jolted Tyler upright. He'd already snoozed his alarm once. This time the stupid musical tune cutting through the house was his cell phone.

He glanced at Kate, who slept on, before he hopped out of bed and ran into the kitchen. He retrieved his cell phone from where he'd left it on the counter and snapped it open. "Tyler Nichols."

"Ty." Jess didn't even waste a breath. "Get in here pronto. The situation in—" Jess named an African country "—has blown again and Banta's asking for you."

"Now's not a good time, Jess," he responded, experiencing a pang of remorse as he thought of Kate lying in his bed. "I promised my mother I'd try to be home for Christmas." *And Kate and I made plans to go Christmas shopping and spend the weekend together and...*

"Christmas is Tuesday. Today's Friday. I should be able to get you home in time."

"I *have* to be home. Being out of the country is not an option this year."

"This situation's not an option, either. Banta's rebel troops have hostages and they've set off ten car bombs, killing at least fifty people. The rebellion is a bloody mess and we'll be lucky to get you and Thomas in before the airport is seized. You did that photo essay on Banta last year. You're our ace in the hole. The world needs to know what he's planning."

"I…" Tyler paused and stared at his free hand as if it were a foreign object. Normally, his adrenaline would be pumping and his blood racing. Once, when Jess had phoned, he'd left a woman in the midst of having sex. He'd lost all interest in everything but the assignment Jess had presented him with.

So why was he now arguing with his assignment editor? The answer, when it came, floored him. Because he'd changed.

Jess sensed his indecision. "Ty, you're it. The one Banta wants. You know the country well enough to stay safe, and Clay's wife just had a baby. I can't send him into the fray. You'll be home in time, and if you do this, I promise I won't send you out of the state for a month. How's that?"

Tyler didn't want to leave Kate. Not now, after they'd been as close as two people could get. Damn, he'd been bitten. *He loved her.* His leaving, even if it was his job, would disappoint her, and frankly, he couldn't abide that. Nora's warning rang in his ears. *You're going to break her heart.*

Jess must have realized his turmoil. "Please, Tyler," she pleaded. "Home by Christmas."

She'd had him home for Kate's party. He knew Banta better than the other photographers. He and Thomas were the best ones for this assignment.

"I'm on my way." Tyler hit the end button on the cell phone. Home by Christmas. Then he'd arrange something permanent so that he wouldn't have to be apart from Kate. He didn't want to travel, not when his relationship was at a turning point. For the first time, he suddenly had something to lose.

Kate was awake and sitting when he returned to the bedroom. "Hey," she said. "What's going on?" She saw his expression and the light in her eyes faded.

He leaned down and kissed her. Her lips were sweet, and still swollen from their earlier passion. "Change of plans on my end. I've got to go in to work. I'm being sent back to Africa."

"Oh."

Tyler sat next to her. "I hate to leave like this, but I'm the only one who can go. I've dealt with Banta before—he's the rebel leader. I can get access to him that others can't."

"You're going into a rebel camp," Kate said.

"It's not like what you see in the movies," Tyler said, trying to reassure her. Well, it was close, but not exactly. However, Kate would only fret if she knew the details. He stood and grabbed the suitcase he always had readied for situations like this. "I'll call you, if I can, when I get there. Whatever you do, don't stress if you don't hear from me. No news is always good news. I'll be home by Christmas. Jess said so."

With that, he leaned down and kissed her thoroughly. "I'm going to miss you." And then he was gone, the Hummer creating a distinctive roar as he drove off.

Kate remained in the rumpled bed for several long minutes, uncaring that she was going to be late for work. His work interfering hadn't taken long, had it? He'd made love to her all night, and now he'd left. Loneliness invaded her and she struggled to shake off the melancholy. Tyler had promised to be home by Christmas.

She quickly dressed. Then, heart heavy, she locked Tyler's door and crossed the short distance to her house.

Nora was outside picking up the morning paper, and seeing Kate, she waved and walked over. The eyes behind the cat-eye glasses narrowed as she drew closer. Kate stood rooted to the spot. Time for another moment of truth.

"He broke your heart, didn't he?" Nora said without preamble.

Her direct words shattered Kate's resolve. Tyler had gone to Africa. Behind enemy lines. Fear unlike any she'd known punched her. "No. My heart's not broken." Her lips quivered, but she wouldn't cry. He'd said Christmas. She had to trust him.

"I told him he would," Nora said. "The day of your windows. I warned both of you."

Kate didn't need to hear any of this now. "He just got called to Africa. He's going into a rebel camp. I'm worried. That's all."

"I told him he'd always be gone. I warned that man not to mess with you."

"Nora, I know you mean well, but not now," Kate snapped. She'd never spoken this brusquely to Nora, and the older lady's eyes widened.

Then understanding dawned. "You love him, don't you?"

Kate nodded. "Yes, I do."

"Oh, honey." Nora stepped forward and gave Kate a hug. "I'm sorry if I'm harsh. I worry about you. You're like my own daughter. I only want you happy."

"What if something happens? What if he doesn't come home?" Kate asked, concern weighing her. Perhaps this was how military spouses felt. All she knew was that a black cloud had descended.

"Of course he'll be back. He's good at his job. You'll see him again. Christmas, he said?"

Kate sighed. "Yes."

"Then he'll be home."

But in the end, Christmas came and went, and Tyler never returned.

Chapter Fifteen

Worrying was futile. If there were any lessons to be learned from this, it was that no matter what you wished for, Santa didn't always bring it.

Not even the arrival of her houseguests and Niles, who turned out not to be anywhere as geeky as Frieda had portrayed him, could divert Kate's attention as Christmas Eve approached. She watched CNN, checked the newspapers and Web sites for Tyler's bylined photos.

She'd broken down late Christmas Eve and phoned Tara. "Don't worry, Kate," Tara had told her. "This is nothing new. Tyler's often gone for weeks at a time. A two-day job turns into ten, that sort of thing. If anything's wrong, we'll know immediately because his employer will call us long before the news hits the media. You just hang in there and have a great holiday."

That Tyler did this often didn't make Kate feel better. She checked her e-mail several times an hour. She checked her answering machine and voice mail obsessively, afraid she'd missed a call. She tried his cell-phone number, but immediately got his voice mail, as if his phone had been turned off. She didn't leave a message, afraid it might make her look like the needy fool and basket case she'd become.

"You should take a break, dear," Nora told her two days after Christmas while they were braving the postholiday shopping crowds.

"I agree with your assessment. I'm breaking up with him," Kate declared, her nerves fraught from days of dealing with the unknown. "I can't do this. I can't be in a relationship where I worry if he's even alive because he's in some rebel camp."

"I've been following the news," Nora said. "It's the top story and not a good situation."

"Tell me something I don't know," Kate said.

"You need to get some rest and relaxation, especially since your houseguests don't appear to be leaving."

"*Your* guests," Kate pointed out.

"Don't remind me," Nora said. "I didn't think they'd plan to stay well into the new year. They said they were going back yesterday, but here they are. Listen. Why don't you go somewhere? Cindy has a condo on the beach. The least she could do is give you the keys while she's living at your place and annoying me. Why don't you head there for the weekend and come back New Year's Day?"

"That might be a good idea," Kate agreed. "I'm constantly looking out my window to see if Tyler's driving up."

"Some fresh sea air might do you a world of good," Nora said. "Get your mind off Dogwood Lane and its memories for a while."

"The office *is* closed this week," Kate conceded.

"So you have time to take a minivacation," Nora insisted. "I'll discuss it with Cindy as soon as we get back. She owes you for outwearing her welcome. Now, what do you think about this? It's seventy-five percent off."

Nora held up a box with an inflatable gingerbread man. When set up in a yard, he'd stand seven feet tall. Kate glanced at the picture on the box. "Uh, tacky?"

"Perfect," Nora said. "He's only twenty-five bucks. He'll be my focal point in next year's holiday decorations. Come on, I'll buy you lunch."

THE FIRST INDICATION that anything had changed on Dogwood Lane during the time he'd been away was the strange car in Kate's driveway. The second was a huge inflatable gingerbread man standing front and center in Nora's yard.

Tyler drove the Hummer up under the carport. It was the afternoon of New Year's Eve, and he was finally out of the godforsaken, war-torn country he'd been sent to.

Some Christmas this had turned out to be. Only hours after he'd arrived in the tiny African nation, Banta's forces had seized the airport. Tyler's crew had survived the gunshots, only to be "captured" by the rebels, who'd finally understood enough to take him to their leader.

Once in the rebel encampment, Tyler had been unable to make unsupervised contact with the outside world. His cell phone had been removed, and his laptop confiscated. He'd only been allowed to upload his pictures via satellite feed once they'd been "inspected" and approved. Thomas's copy had suffered the same indignities.

For the most part, both men had existed in a vacuum, cut off from the rest of the world. Because shelling was frequent, Banta moved often, dragging Tyler and Thomas with him. Tyler shook his head and entered his house.

He'd been caught up in a turf war where love, and the beauty of it, didn't exist; only survival did. He'd been in such a situation on many occasions, but this time he'd hated it; felt no thrill. He'd only wanted to go home.

Tyler ran a finger across the kitchen table. A light layer of dust had settled over everything, signaling that he needed to clean. He hadn't yet hired a service or even gotten around to changing the furnace filters.

He glanced around, assessing everything. Had it been just a month since he'd moved in and gotten to know Kate during a cleaning party? He'd missed her something fierce. He'd kept himself going by dreaming of her and the future he was determined they'd have. He wanted to see her, give her the Black Forest music box he'd found in the airport gift shop during his layover.

He'd yearned for her, and his longing had multiplied every day of his absence. Her photos had still been on his camera's memory card, and her beauty and grace had been the only positive thing for him in a country gone to hell....

After a shower and a change into fresh clothes, Tyler prepared to see Kate. He went over to her kitchen and knocked. The door opened a crack, stopped by the security chain.

The elderly lady who answered frowned at him. "I'm not buying anything."

Tyler stared at her. "I'm looking for Kate. She lives here."

"Not this week." The woman's face creased in suspicion and immediately Tyler's nerves were on full alert. Kate hadn't mentioned having company.

He glanced around. He was on the right street, wasn't he? Was he in an episode of the *Twilight Zone?* "Look,

I'm Tyler Nichols. I live next door. Kate and I are dating."

"Do you have any identification?" The woman's gaze remained on his, her hands out of sight behind the door. Tyler wondered if she had a weapon of some sort trained on him.

"My driver's license is in my house, which is right over there." He pointed toward his kitchen. "Could you please just tell me where Kate is?"

"No." With that, the woman slammed the door shut and Tyler heard the lock click.

For a long moment Tyler stood in Kate's driveway, aware that the woman watched him from behind the curtains. Tyler felt like banging on the door again and demanding an answer, but if the woman was anything like Nora, she probably had 911 on speed dial.

Nora. Of course Nora would know what was going on. Tyler jogged across the street and knocked on her door.

"Ah, the prodigal son returns," Nora said in greeting as she opened the door wide. "I've been waiting for you to head over. I guess you met Patti."

"Was that who slammed the door in my face?"

"She shares my safe habits, and you're letting my heat out." Nora gestured for him to enter. "One can't be too careful these days, you know. No one's very trustworthy anymore."

That was definitely a dig at him.

"I thought you'd be back by Christmas," Nora said as Tyler stepped inside.

"I ran into a little trouble. Is Patti one of Kate's relatives?"

Nora's eyes narrowed and she pushed her glasses back up on her nose. "No."

Oh, this was not good. Hadn't he just been through hell? "Is she a friend?" Tyler inquired.

Nora picked at a loose thread on an afghan thrown over the back of a chair. "No."

"Nora, please." Tyler's frustration mounted.

Nora let out an exaggerated sigh. Tyler checked his temper. The infernal woman was actually enjoying this. "It's really very simple," Nora said. "Patti is my relative. She came to visit, and Kate put her and Cindy up. Kate went to the beach."

"She what?" Tyler stopped pacing and stared at Nora. "Why would she do that?"

"Because someone didn't call or return the way he promised he would. Instead he loved her and left her. You broke her heart and she needed some time to heal."

The room grew silent as Tyler digested the implications. "I told her no news was good news," he said.

"Kate's not from your world," Nora snapped. "She worried. She constantly watched the news, something she never does. I told you that you would hurt her."

Without his cell phone, Tyler hadn't been able to phone his family or Kate. He'd gotten out of bed and deserted her for work the moment Jess called. He'd always told Kate his job was his mistress. Even though he'd ditched the governor to be with her, that really didn't prove anything.

She believed his job was too dangerous. Too important. And knowing Kate, she wouldn't be able to love a man whose employment kept him constantly traveling. No, Kate needed security, and Tyler and his job weren't that. His knees weakened, and he sat on Nora's brocade sofa.

"Would you like some tea?" Nora asked politely.

"No, I'm fine," he lied. He ran a hand through his hair, which was starting to dry.

Nora perched primly on the end of her love seat. She reached for the teapot and poured herself a cup. Steam wafted as she made him wait. "Are you certain you wouldn't like some? When I saw you arrive, I put out a cup for you."

"No, thank you." He drew himself up. He had to find out what was going on. "About Kate. Did I hear you correctly? She's at the beach?"

"Your ears are working fine," Nora confirmed. "Cindy has a condo. I suggested that Kate take some time to relax. She hasn't had a break in what amounts to forever, and with your absence, she's been despondent. You told her you'd be here, and even your sister told her not to fret. But Kate stresses. She—"

"Nora." Without worrying if it was rude, Tyler interrupted her spiel. He cared about Kate. *He loved her.*

"Nora," Tyler repeated, searching for the perfect words. "I need your help. I need to get in touch with her."

"No." Nora sipped her tea and looked over the teacup at him.

"No?" Tyler stared at Nora.

"I already told you that your ears are working fine. I said no. You leave Kate alone. She must arrive at her own decision about you. She'll be home soon enough. Late tomorrow, I'm assuming."

"I need to see her now," Tyler said.

"Not going to happen. You let me know if there's

anything else I can do for you, Tyler," Nora said. "We watch out for each other on this block."

Yeah, sure you do, Tyler thought as he walked across the street to his house. He tried Kate's cell phone, but she didn't answer, and her voice mail picked up immediately.

He'd made it into the house when his cell phone started trilling. He looked at the number. "Hey, Tara."

"You rang. I'm returning your call."

Don't sound so friendly. "Yeah. I'm back in town. Thanks for watching the house. Everything appears fine. How upset is Mom that I missed Christmas?"

"She's not happy. You risk too much," Tara chided him, her tone unforgiving.

He did take too many chances. He realized that now. "You won't believe what happened to me—"

She cut him off. "It's always something."

"Yeah, being trapped by rebels is a big something." Tyler calmed himself. His twin was correct. His job did come with its full share of Murphy's Law fiascos. *Something* always went wrong. "Have you talked to Kate?"

"Not since she left for the beach."

So Tara had been in contact with Kate. "Where exactly is she?" he asked.

"I'm not being dragged into the middle of this," Tara said.

"You already are. I want to see her." Tyler paced his kitchen and bit the bullet. Only one declaration would convince Tara to help. "I love her."

Dead silence from his sister.

"Are you there?" he demanded, afraid he'd lost her cell-phone signal.

"Yes," she said.

"It's New Year's Eve. You're supposed to be with the person you love tonight. You know, start the year off right. Tell me where she is."

"She may not want to see you," Tara said, and Tyler waited as his twin contemplated his revelation.

"I'll risk Kate's wrath," Tyler said. "Just tell me she's not too far away and that I can get there in time."

He heard Tara inhale sharply as she wrestled with her decision. "I love her, Tara. I want to marry her. Have you ever heard me say either? The flowers weren't a fluke."

"You'll never be home," she argued weakly.

"That's changing, too. Just tell me."

Another silence, this one not as long as the first, and his sister caved. "Okay," Tara said finally. "Get a pen."

KATE OPENED her car door and stared at the two plastic bags sitting on the seat. Tonight would be her last night at the beach, so she'd splurged on carryout from a local restaurant, then stopped at the quick mart on the way home, where she'd bought ice cream and a half-size bottle of champagne. The champagne had been an impulse purchase. She didn't even know if she'd open it. She really didn't feel like celebrating. All New Year's Eve did was remind you to make resolutions you wouldn't keep and that you would turn another year older, with only a job to show for your efforts.

Kate gripped the plastic bags as she began climbing the stairs. Cindy's condo was on the third floor of a building without an elevator.

She set the bags down on the landing and inserted her key in the lock. She backed in, holding the door open with her rear, before setting the bags inside on the floor. With a groan of exasperation, she moved out of the door's way as it slammed shut with an ominous click.

"You know, you really ought to look first. No telling who might have wandered in off the street."

"Augh!" Kate shrieked, her hands flailing at the voice. She saw him immediately, sitting on the couch. "Tyler!"

"Hello, Kate." He stood up and stretched, his gaze never leaving her face. "It's good to see you."

"What are you doing here? How did you get in?" Kate reached for the door handle, anything, to calm the emotions rocketing through her. He appeared thinner and more drawn, as if he'd been without sleep for a few nights.

He shrugged. "Your house has much better locks. That poor excuse for a dead bolt took me approximately two minutes to jimmy. I've been waiting for you for over an hour. I've missed you."

Total disbelief. Did he really think mere words could make everything better? Kate tried to explain things rationally. "You didn't come home and I—" Suddenly, her jaw dropped. The condo was covered in roses. Red roses. Pink roses. White ones. She clenched her hands to get control.

"Happy New Year, Kate," he said. "I missed Christmas. I'm so sorry."

She shook her head. "This is too much. You can't just waltz in here and—"

"Yes, I can," he interrupted. "I'm not losing you again. I've been trapped in a foreign country behind enemy lines, wanting nothing more than to be with you. When I got home, the first person I went to see was you. You have every right to be angry with me. I left you in my bed. I promised to come back and I didn't. I'll pay for that the rest of my life, that I swear to you."

"It doesn't matter. There's no sense rehashing what happened. It's okay, it's forgotten and I've decided to move on. You and I are good in bed. I can't handle your travel. This isn't going to work."

"Kate, I planned to be here. I'll spare you the unpleasantness of what my experience being trapped was like. Just know that you were always on my mind. We are meant to work this out. Why else would fate have put me next door to you if not to meet you?"

She stood still, waiting and watching.

"I'm through leaving, and I'm not about to let either of us run away from how we feel about each other. You're the best thing that's ever happened to me and you're not getting rid of me."

"I can always call the police," she whispered, knowing deep in her heart she wouldn't do anything of the sort. She loved him. Yet her pride dictated she fight, despite the roses everywhere.

Tyler inched closer. "I pulled some strings on the way back. Hard to do considering that it's New Year's Eve, but from here on out, I'm local to Orlando. Very little, if any, travel, and that travel is not to be dangerous. Ever."

"I thought you loved to travel. Work being your mistress and all that." Kate eyed him suspiciously. Roses and now this declaration. Did she dare hope?

"Perhaps it was, but I'd rather have you. You see, I used to think travel was everything—until I met you. When I was away, all I could think of was getting back home. That morning after Jess called, I decided to do one last job before asking for a permanent stateside assignment. I never intended to leave you alone. You are the best thing about my life. You've captured my entire focus."

"Oh, Tyler."

She stepped forward, and he frowned and pointed. "Something's leaking out of the bag. Do you need to put that away?"

"Oh, my ice cream! I bought that and some champagne."

"Planning a party?"

"A pity party, more like it," Kate admitted, carrying the bag into the kitchen. "I was going to ring in the new year with the TV."

She put the leaking container in the freezer. The kitchen became even tinier when she realized Tyler had followed her.

"It'll refreeze," she told him.

"Good." He crowded her. "Do you know how much I've missed you?" He touched her hair. "You are so beautiful. So refreshing. So perfect. You're most definitely your own person. That's one of the things I love about you."

He'd just said that was one of the things he loved about her. Kate jerked up, and almost bashed her head on the cabinet.

"Careful, darling." He reached out and guided her to him. "I don't want anything to happen to you. Do you know how often I pictured you while I was gone? You were with me in my dreams, when I ate, everywhere. I even had your photos on my camera. They kept me going. You were my hope, my strength."

"Tyler, I…"

"Shh. Let me talk." He put a finger to her lips. It was an intimate gesture, and Kate fell silent. "Like I said, the first thing I did when I returned home was go to your house. Instead of you, I found Patti. She wasn't a pleasant surprise, believe me. Next I went to see Nora, who read me the riot act about breaking your heart. She refused to even tell me where you'd gone."

"She can be pretty stubborn," Kate stated.

His brown eyes narrowed and he studied her for a moment. When he spoke, his voice was tender. "Kate, I want nothing more than to be with you from here on out. I'd planned on being home by Christmas, telling you I loved you and asking you to marry me. Needless to say, I wasn't expecting to be trapped in Africa. That made things complicated, so let me make everything clear. I love you."

"You love me?"

He smiled warmly at her, a grin that began to erase all her deepest fears. "Absolutely, I love you. I never wanted to be your fake date. Even from the beginning, I wanted to be so much more. That night we made love, I knew I loved you. I planned on telling you when I got back. I guess I'm a little late."

"You love me." Raw happiness flooded Kate's heart.

"Forever and ever. Out in the living room is a present."

"That's sweet."

"You can see it later. In just a minute, if that's okay. I'm still not satisfied."

Her happiness prickled a little. She'd never seen Tyler so serious, so determined. "You're not?"

"Oh, no." Tyler shook his head. "This time, Kate, I want more than just to be your boyfriend. This time I want it all. To be your husband, who loves you until death parts us, to be the father of your children. I want to be the one who will defeat your demons, or at least be behind you, guarding your back while you slay them. I don't ever want to be separated from you again."

His words overwhelmed her and Kate leaned back against the kitchen counter for support. She'd never been so, well, happy. "I, Tyler, I don't know what to say."

"Say you love me. You do love me, don't you, Kate?" He appeared worried, and she put a hand on his cheek.

"I do love you," she said. "So very much. I fretted obsessively while you were gone. I checked the news media every hour. Nora insisted I get away."

"Shh. It's okay. I'm settled, Kate. I've a job in town, a house that's on the street you love. Most of all, I love you. I think we can make this work."

"Oh, Tyler." In an instant he closed the remaining few inches separating them and gathered her into his arms.

"I love you, Kate Merrill," he said, a bit more forcefully this time. "You are my life, my love. Be my wife."

"I will," Kate said as he rained kisses down. Happiness was found in his wonderful arms, and for the longest time she just kissed him and reveled in the glory of his touch.

He drew back for a moment. "So you'll marry me?"

"I will. But don't break in on me anymore. You almost gave me a heart attack."

He grinned. "Then I accomplished my purpose," he said before he dropped two quick kisses on her nose. "You see, I wanted you to know I'm the only one who can fix your heart, the way you've fixed mine. You've filled a hole inside me. You make me complete. Completely happy, completely in love, completely crazy."

No further words were spoken as Tyler captured Kate's mouth again and they savored each other's kisses for several minutes. Kate basked in the glow of loving Tyler, the man she'd waited to find.

"We'll have to call my mother and Tara later," Tyler murmured. "Tara's the one who told me where you were."

"I'm glad. We wouldn't be doing this if she hadn't."

"I guess I'll owe her a favor," Tyler said.

"We both will. I love you," she said.

Tyler nuzzled her earlobe. "If you know how much I've longed to hear you say those three words. Tell me again."

"I love you."

"Show me," he whispered, and when he led her toward the bedroom, Kate followed him willingly. He loved her until both were too exhausted to move, meaning that when the condo community shot off fireworks at midnight to celebrate the new year, they simply watched from bed. The fireworks burst into brilliant light over the ocean and Kate curled into Tyler's arms, perfectly content. A while ago he'd given her the most beautiful snow globe and a music box. He'd had to wipe the tears of happiness from her eyes before they'd made love again.

"Kate?"

"Yes?" He'd started tracing circles on her arm and he leaned close to her as the fireworks finale began.

"Happy New Year. You're supposed to kiss the one you love at midnight. Want to hear my resolution first?"

"What's that?"

"To love you forever," he said.

And as the fireworks reached their booming crescendo, with a kiss the future began.

Epilogue

When the wedding came to an end, Frieda dabbed her eyes with a handkerchief. She'd never been to a lovelier ceremony than that of Kate Merrill and Tyler Nichols. All the residents of Dogwood Lane had turned out for the June nuptials, hosted at Marshall and Laverne Evans's estate.

Since both Tyler and Kate lived on Dogwood Lane, no one from the block had known exactly which side of the aisle to sit on. In the end, after Nora had made a point of sitting on Kate's side, Frieda had decided to join her. After all, much to Nora's chagrin, Frieda was witnessing the permanent love match she'd predicted that night of cleaning, a match that had survived despite Nora's well-intentioned meddling.

"Cheer up, Nora," Frieda said as Kate finished her vows and kissed her handsome groom. "After all, Niles is marrying a divorcée with three kids."

"Hmmph," Nora snorted as the pastor presented the newly married couple to the guests. Frieda grinned. Nora wasn't too happy about her grandson's choice, but at least she'd accepted it. Both women hushed as the bride and groom kissed again.

Kate was all smiles as she and Tyler walked down the

aisle on their first journey as husband and wife. Sunlight beamed through the tree canopy and Frieda put her handkerchief away and sighed with contentment. Kate had it all. She'd finished law school, accepted a position at Marshall's firm and married the man of her dreams. Tyler had kept his word and now handled only local news. He was also publishing a retrospective of his photographs.

Frieda sensed a hand on her shoulder and turned, but no one was there. "She's fine, Sandra," Frieda whispered to the wind. "You can rest now. She's just fine."

Because with Tyler's love, Frieda knew that for the rest of Kate's days, Kate would be exactly that.

* * * * *